TEENAGE LIFE.... ALONG SOMEONE

Sometimes...someone...when and how comes in your life, who cares with you, loves you....you will never feel and realise but you run behind another unknown without any expectation.

BY.... ABHISHEK TRIHOTREE

BLUEROSE PUBLISHERS
India | U.K.

Copyright © Abhishek Trihotree 2024

All rights reserved by author. No part of this publication may be reproduced, stored in a retrieval system or transmitted in any form or by any means, electronic, mechanical, photocopying, recording or otherwise, without the prior permission of the author. Although every precaution has been taken to verify the accuracy of the information contained herein, the publisher assumes no responsibility for any errors or omissions. No liability is assumed for damages that may result from the use of information contained within.

BlueRose Publishers takes no responsibility for any damages, losses, or liabilities that may arise from the use or misuse of the information, products, or services provided in this publication.

For permissions requests or inquiries regarding this publication, please contact:

BLUEROSE PUBLISHERS
www.BlueRoseONE.com
info@bluerosepublishers.com
+91 8882 898 898
+4407342408967

ISBN: 978-93-6261-535-0

Cover design: Shivam
Typesetting: Namrata Saini

First Edition: August 2024

Contents

Introduction 1

Chapter-1: Beginning of the Journey 3

Chapter-2: Terrible Night with Her 27

Chapter-3: Birth of a Beautiful Friendship 38

Chapter-4: Expectations, Wishes and the Beautiful Gift 53

Chapter-5: College Lifestyle and The Journey with Her 90

Chapter-6: Mission Accomplished 115

Chapter-7: Shadows of Addiction 122

Chapter-8: Fighting Darkness and Meeting the Light of My Life 142

Introduction

Welcome to my "**TEENAGE LIFE...Along Someone**". In this book.... some parts are observations and some parts are imaginations.

My name is **ABHISHEK TRIHOTREE**, from *Muzaffarpur, Bihar*. In this book, I travelled different states of India like...**Bihar** to **Rajasthan**, **Rajasthan** to **Delhi-NCR**. It took me five years to complete this **Teenage Life** and met **someone**.

The journey of the Teenage years, I dedicate this book for my Teenage self who wanted to be an **Engineer** and my character's name is **Kumar Siddhartha**. What can you say about me; you will get to know very well and very soon when you read this story....

But one thing I want to tell about me. Might be, I supposed to myself......and I was thinking, "**I'm that toughest question of maths, where people first don't understand me easily, and that's why anyone doesn't want to understand me. If any case....if anyone wants to understand, do you know....what happens...? Time is an idiot......! (Laughing......!); It's over, and that's what I am.**"

I mean....**I'm neither dumb nor deaf but like to speak very little, the real reason is that I don't even know to speak enough and since my childhood I wanted to live alone not in a group because I don't know...why? However, I wanted to keep myself in groups; but sometimes in a group if any person said**

anything that was not acceptable to me, then I would have been out of the group. Due to my lack of speaking habit, I was not able to explain my words properly, due to which, I was getting rejection from many places.

Actually, if a person comes to talk to me, then I feel very comfortable and happily talk to him/her, but when I want to talk first time to an unknown or known person, then while going towards that person, I start to think, "**The person will be ready to talk me or not?**" This thinking got me very nervous and, hence, I would retract my steps. Of course, I needed a best friend. But I was scared and I didn't like anyone making fun of me because of my shortcomings. That's why I always liked to stay away from people.

But this did not continue for long. One day, someone suddenly came into my life.....actually....it was my fault that I could not give enough time to me to understand and know to myself. But she proved me and my thinking.... wrong, she knew and understood me instantly that I couldn't even know......!

Chapter-1

Beginning of the Journey

It was during the period when I appeared for my 12th board examination. After that examination, I wanted to apply for The Joint Entrance Examination (JEE). As you know that it is a national level exam which is conducted to get into engineering colleges. JEE occurs in two phases: JEE Main and JEE Advance.

You cannot apply for the JEE Advance without passing the JEE Main. So, I first applied for JEE Main and appeared for the exam.

But after the examination, when my RESULTS were announced, I found that the results were not at par with my expectations. Because of it, I could not be selected for JEE Advance. However, I did not lose my hope and I thought that if I was given another chance then I would have performed better.

So, I thought that let me first talk to my father in this connection. And I talked to him, "Papa! I want to prepare for this examination once again. I hope that I would perform better than before."

Papa said, "That's okay, if you think, you want to prepare again, okay....go ahead."

And he added, "Where do you want to go for preparation and have you searched anywhere….?"

I excitedly smiled and said, "Thank you so much Papa…! And yes I will inform you as soon as possible…!"

My father said, "Okay…no issues, take your time…!"

Then, I searched on Google and also discussed with my senior about the best institute. After collecting all information, I informed to my father that I wanted to go to Kota. *(I think, I don't need to explain because you may have heard of it. If not, it is located in Rajasthan and also known as Kota Factory for the exam preparation. Because, students from every corner of India go there to prepare for JEE-Main Exam, like Mukherjee Nagar, Delhi is known for Civil Service Exam.)*

My father said, "Okay….!"

Finally I enrolled for coaching in Kota with the help of some person and started living in a Hostel.

Here was a new place, a new class and new students totally unknown for me. I didn't know anyone. That was the time, I was miles away from my home. But I was also very excited about to know new environment.

In that institute, there was a system that anyone, either boy or girl, could sit anywhere or together, but they had to reserve their seat first, as per their choice, provided that seat was vacant.

At the beginning, a boy used to sit beside me always; but after some days, he did not come in my class; perhaps he changed his class or was absent for some reason, I didn't know about it.

One day when I entered into the class and started to sit on the seat, I saw a new student **sitting beside me but she was a girl. I didn't know her name. Obviously how could I know?**

I saw her for the first time, she was looking very gorgeous.

For some reason or the other, I wanted to look at her again and again, at her beautiful pink lips (she didn't use lipstick, but without using lipstick her lips were pink).

Sometimes, I wanted to look at her black beautiful eyes (she did not used much makeup, only she used very little black colour in her eyes); I kept wanting to look at her again and again.

I didn't know she knew or not about me that I was noticing all activities and looking at her but when she looked at towards me I started behaving like...I didn't look at her and kept busy in studies to look like a very serious student.

When she was copying from the blackboard and while writing, she spoke slowly with her lips vibrating. I was very confused about which one was very beautiful....her pink lips or her black beautiful eyes. I smiled and thought...and I didn't have the answer. But I knew that I was deeply attracted towards her.

Before, neither I sat with a girl too close nor studied in co-education school or college. That's why, first; I felt very uncomfortable and disturbed. But gradually I started busying myself to look at her activities and tried to behave well in front of her.

For that way I also started going too far from my studies. Because of it, I wasn't focusing on studies and tried to do unknown activities so that she looked towards me and smile.

Without wanting, I saw her directly or indirectly again and again.

Sometimes I was feeling, "Why am I here? I mean…. I'm not here for the stupid things in that way I'm totally wasting my time."

So, I decided to speak with her and told her to leave that seat. Many times I told her but she refused every time. One day, at the lunch time she met me then I told her about the same.

Do you know what…she told me?

She replied, "First you tell me…what problem do you have…?"

I smiled and said, "No I don't have any problem but I just want you to leave the seat. Before you….my friend used to sit there. (Actually, he was not my friend and I just knew him. But I lied that he was my friend so that she can leave the seat.)"

Thereafter, she told me, "If you have any problem then you can change your seat but not me."

That was too much for me. But due to some issues I was absent next day, so after the next day I wrote something in my Notebook and asked her first, "Yesterday, did any boy sit here…?"

She said, "No and why….?"

I replied, "Nothing…!"

Then I gave her my notebook and told her to read it now, what I wrote in notebook. She looked towards me doubtfully. I replied, "You don't worry, just read it."

Thereafter, she started reading. And that was….,

"Please don't mind. But you don't want that I would like to sit here. Because..., when you sit here. I start feeling very uncomfortable and felt disturbing to myself. I'm also not studying well. That's why I told you before and many times for leaving this seat but you refused every time. That's why I decided to tell all things clearly so that you don't mind.

When two days ago you didn't come to sit here, I felt very happy and very comfortable, and was studying very well."

She was laughing while reading this but I didn't know that what she was thinking? After reading she returned my notebook.

Again she asked me to give that notebook. Because, that day she was sitting with her friend and she gave it to her friend for reading. She started reading and both started laughing. First girl who seated along me she started beating her friend and was also laughing.

Thereafter, I smiled and told her to read next page, where I wrote something more on the next page. And that was......,

"When I look at your beautiful eyes. They are really very pretty and deeply attractive to me. You know that I'm a boy and I have also a lot of feeling about the girl. So please, please don't mind. Because I also have a problem, if I don't tell you these things then I start feeling unwell. But you once read it, I will feel good. Thank you...!"

After reading this, she returned me the Notebook. She stood and told her friend to exchange her seat. Then I felt embarrassed, so I smiled and said to her, "You don't need to exchange your seat. So, you don't worry....!"

She smiled and asked, "Are you sure, you wouldn't have any problem. If I sit here...?"

I smiled and said, "Yes, please you can sit here, I don't have any problem now." I felt very relaxed after sharing my feelings.

But, I didn't know what she was thinking about me.....

However, sometimes her face expression was not good about me. I looked at her, she was laughing and of course she was laughing. Because I just did something that was laughable but I was not sure, what she was thinking, when I saw her face expression; she might be thinking, "He is totally mad and an idiot."

Or might be, she was thinking, "What a silly boy...?",

or might be anything more and I didn't know.

But that day, after attending two classes, suddenly she went. I didn't know....why...?

On the other hand, I kept feeling so embarrassed to tell her. And the next day for some reason, she didn't come. That way, my doubt increased. Then I started feeling too bad and thought, "How would I get to look at her?"

Therefore, I decided, "Now, I do not talk and look at her, I will also not ever let her feel that I like her."

She came after some days; when she entered into the class and sat at the same place, where she used to sit before.

After that if she did any kind of activities. I didn't see. Before if she did any types of activities like laughing, doing fun with her friend, so I used to look at her and I felt happy to see her and sometimes I also started silently laughing to see her naughty activities and was feeling enjoy. That's why I liked her.

But from the day (when I shared with her my feelings.) thereafter, I started distancing her and from the day didn't look towards her. When sometimes whether she asked anything or did any kind of naughty behaviours. First, I didn't talk her like before even if I spoke, it was with anger and asked her to stop it and saw her to make my face angry. I used to present myself as very rude to her.

Because I was thinking, "Lest she start thinking that I am harassing her."

But despite the fact that…..

Of course I kept stopping myself for going towards her, talking with her, looking towards her, thinking about her.

But sometimes I wanted to go ahead and towards her and talked with her a lot, every time and every moment, I wanted to see her again and again, wanted to be part of my life and made her my whole world.

I did not know…how…? But sometime I felt like that someone pushed me to go ahead and went towards her and said sorry about my aggressive behaviour, about all things and sometime I felt like that someone said to me stop it and pulled to stop me and didn't go to talk her.

I thought, "May be, because of me."

Actually…of course, we didn't talk to each other but whenever I entered into my class, before sitting, first of all I looked at her seat to know whether she came or not. After sitting on my place, I again used to look at her and it became my habit to do so.

One day, when I entered into my class and went to sit at my place, while going to sit, my first sight went to her place where she used to sit before. I sat and when I didn't see beside me at her place then I searched everywhere in the class.

Might be she was absent at that day for any issues. But when I got to know that she didn't come then I started finding her everywhere but she did not meet me, thereafter, I went to sit and thought that might be, she had some problem that's why she was not coming. I tried to make myself understand but failed and at that day, I didn't feel good and didn't study well.

But again, next day....when I arrived and entered into the class. I saw and was surprised because she had come before me and was laughing (not on me) as well as talking to her friend. Thereafter, I went to go to my seat and took a deep breath and closed my eyes and said to God, "Thank God to see her again."

Many times I tried to know her name. So one day when she went outside for lunch with her friend, then I took her notebooks and started finding her name, but I couldn't because she didn't write her name on any of her notebooks.

Gradually, I started loving her a lot. If any boy said anything about her or passed any kind of vulgar comment in front of me, sometimes I refused to listen, sometimes I told them to stop saying anything about her indirectly and sometimes went away from there.

Many times I felt like fighting or killing them, if anybody told anything about her but I didn't do that. I didn't have any purpose for fighting because she was not mine at the time.

When my heart started thinking about her, about taking care of her then I was sure that I started loving her and I really loved her.

But without knowing about her, I couldn't take rest.

First, I tried to know her casual friend (not her best friend, the friend who went to meet her regularly and talk to her, yet she was not like her best friend). Because if I asked about her to her best friend then at the any cost her best friend would tell her.

That's why I started searching and noticing, who met her regular outside or inside the class.

I noticed and found out a girl, who used to meet her often for some work and sometimes had lunch with her.

One day I saw, the girl was alone and she was heading outside after finishing the class. I thought of going and talking to her.

But I was little scared, "Is this okay to go and talk to her and ask about the girl who used to sit beside me…?"

I wondered. I felt scared talking to her. How would she react after my asking…?

To think that, my heart started beating faster and the sound was coming outside.

Then I stopped for a moment and thought two or three minutes, I took deep breath two-three times and was trying to relax my mind, but when I saw that she was going then I ran fast and went there where she was.

I started calling, "Excuse me….!"

She stopped and turned back to know who was calling her. She started looking here and there.

I waved my hand and said loudly, "Yes, I'm calling you…., please stop…!"

She stopped with a surprised look.

When I reached to her, she asked, "Why are you calling me…?"

I replied, "Yes…wait…let me relax…! I mean…, I need your help please. That's why I was calling you. So, please…!"

My heart rate was not stopping because I had to run fast and went to be near her.

She asked with a surprise, "Okay…..So….I mean, how can I help you…?"

I said, "You are the only one who can help me, so please help me…!"

After that, she said, "Okay…okay….! Just relax, and but how…?

She said again, "I think…I saw you somewhere. If I'm not wrong, you are my classmate, right…!"

I said, "Yes, exactly…!"

(I thought she might be rude, but I was wrong because she was very nice to talk with me. I think…all girls are nice…but depend on your behaviour.)

She asked me, "So tell me…! How can I help you…?"

I said, "My name is Siddhartha, and yours…?"

She smiled and asked, "Okay…but why…?"

I smiled too and said, "Oh…your name is Okay, nice name…actually very nice…!"

She said, "Of course not…so funny…!"

I smiled and said, "Hey…genuinely you are too much. I asked your name, not your number."

She said, "My name is Anandita Singh Rajput," and we shook hands with each other.

I replied, "Waooo…! Nice name just like you."

Anandita asked, "What…..anyway….whatever you said, but thank you for the compliment….!"

Anandita added, "And that's why, you came here..? To ask my name and compliment…?" and she started laughing.

I said, "No…it's not like that."

She said, "So how is….?"

I quickly said, "Actually, I want to know something about a girl."

Anandita asked, "What….which girl, you are talking about…?"

I replied, "I mean, you know her, the one whom you meet many times in the class; and I want to know her name and to know more about her."

Anandita started smiling and said, "Why, (laughing…..!), why do you want to know about her…?"

I smiled and said, "No-no, don't think anything wrong. I just want to know about her but I am scared to talk to her. You are very nice, so please, please tell me her name and about her!"

Anandita said, "Okay, I understand. But not today, tomorrow at the same time when our class will be over."

I said, "What…and why not now…?"

Anandita said, "Nothing. Do you want to know her name or not?"

I said, "Yes…!"

She replied, "Then keep quiet and meet me at the same time tomorrow."

I smiled and pleaded, "As you wish but don't tell her anything about me, please…!"

She said, "You don't worry," and smiled then she caught an auto, said bye and went away.

The next day, as I entered the classroom I saw Anandita. She too looked at me; we smiled and waved each other. Then I went to sit.

The girl had come already before me and sat at her place. I started smiling to see the girl. Anandita saw me that I was silently looking and smiling to see the girl.

Thereafter, Anandita also started looking towards me. She smiled whenever I looked at the girl. I became happy to see the girl after looking at her.

When the class was over, I went to meet Anandita.

And she told me, "Listen, if I tell her name, so what will you give me? I think, you should give me a small party, I'm too hungry right now."

I requested with folded hands and said, "Okay ma'am, not once, I will give you several parties. But tell me about her."

Anandita smiled and said, "Okay…..so, her name is….!"

I smiled and was waiting to know her name.

She looked at my face and stopped. She started smiling and only smiling.

I asked, "Hey.... you were telling her name, so, why are you pausing now...?"

She smiled and replied, "Because you are smiling and looking so cute while smiling."

She added, "I'm pausing to look at your amazing look and your excitement....it's amazing....!"

I smiled and replied, "Yes, I know. Just forget it, please tell her name...!"

Anandita replied, "Okay...so her name is Mamta; she is very intelligent girl that you know very well, because many times she used to answer questions in the class but I don't know whether she has a boyfriend or not? But if you want some more information then you will have to find out yourself."

When Anandita said her name then I started repeating, "Manu....it is her nice name." and started dreaming too.

Then Anandita kept her hand on my shoulder and said, "Where have you gone...? I told you, her name is Mamta not Manu."

I said, "What difference does it make...? Her name is Mamta or Manu but I want to call her only Manu."

Anandita said again, "Okay-okay whatever I will try to know about her more and you don't worry."

Thereafter, as per her condition we went to a restaurant and had a small party together. After finishing, she took an auto, said bye with enthusiasm and went to her hostel, and I also went.

One day when I entered into the class, Manu didn't come. Second day same thing happened and the third day and so on. My eyes always kept waiting for her.

Many times I asked Anandita why Manu was not coming for some day.

Anandita always replied that she didn't know.

After some days I said to Anandita, "Anandita…will you please help me just one time?"

Anandita replied, "What's the matter tell me first…?"

I said, "If you have Manu's number then please ask her why she is not coming…?"

Anandita replied, "Sorry…I don't have her number."

Then I said, "Will you please ask her friend who always sits with her, about Manu and why she is not coming…? Please you go just one time and ask her why Manu is not coming for the last some days."

Anandita said, "Okay…., you don't worry, leave it to me, I will ask Pallavi."

I asked, "Who is she…?"

"She is Manu's friend; I know her; she always sits with Manu in class as well as lives in the same Hostel," Anandita said.

Anandita asked to Pallavi about Mamta, "Why she is not coming for some days….?"

Pallavi said, "Mamta went to her home for some work and today she will come till evening."

Then Anandita told me everything.

Anandita said again, "But, right now, let's go to eat something, I'm so hungry. Let's go somewhere."

We went to a restaurant, sat safely and said to her, "Anandita….actually…!"

Anandita said, "Actually…what…?"

I said smiling, "Actually…I'm so sorry because I don't have enough money. You have to share some money with me and tomorrow I will return you."

Anandita told me, "You cheater….!"

I laughed and said, "I'm sorry….! And why didn't you tell me before that you will be hungry…?"

She replied, "You…idiot…! I'll get hungry asking you."

I started laughing and said, "Of course…yes…but now I don't have."

She said, "It's okay…, you don't need to give me. My lord please you go and just order now."

I asked her, "What will you prefer?"

She said, "Anything which you want."

I called a waiter and ordered a full plate of Paneer and Veg-Momos and a glass of water.

She was shocked and asked me, "For me, what…?"

I smiled and said, "Please wait…!"

After five minutes, the waiter came with a full plate of Paneer and Veg-Momos and a glass of water. He put it on our table and went.

Then I gave her a glass of water and told her, "This is for you and this dish is for me because you told me that you could eat anything as I want. So please carry on it."

She started laughing and said, "You are so naughty."

I said, "I know."

"But less than me," she said.

And she took my plate and started eating. Then what...?

Those Momos were very hot, even than I also started eating immediately more because she ate very slowly.

We finished it all very soon and I ate more than her. Thereafter, I smiled and asked, "Anything else...?"

She stared at me and said, "Yes, order four Sandwiches but separate, not together...!"

I laughed and said, "Okay...don't worry. I will not eat quickly now."

She said, "Thanks but no need." And I smiled.

Then, she smiled and showed her tongue.

Thereafter, I ordered two-two Sandwiches separately, two for me and two for her. They were very tasty. I wanted to order two more but we were short of money. Despite this, I asked her, "May I order some more...?"

"It is my stomach and not a warehouse (Godam). It's enough for me, pay the bill and let's go now. I want to go somewhere," she said.

I said, "Let me think. Where should we go to feel good?"

She said, "But where...? And first of all, I'm sorry because I don't have money. So...how to manage all things..?"

She said again, "But I'm sorry, I also had only 500 rupees and I have already spent 300 rupees. So I also don't have money, and second thing, I've already forgotten my ATM in my Hostel. I think, it's good, if we should plan for tomorrow…?"

When she was saying this, her face was looking sad but so cute. When, I saw her sad face. I was totally…sorry…!

So, I didn't know…..What…? That was enough for me to convince myself and said to myself, "Anyway just leave it." I started smiling and planning.

I said to her, "Okay, you don't worry. I think…., I've only 200 rupees left in my pocket and I can withdraw only 1000 rupees because two days ago, I withdrew money and this is my father's ATM."

I added, "But you don't worry…today I will try fulfilling your all wishes."

After saying this she kept looking at me for some more time….then started laughing loudly.

(As you know that if a beautiful girl is with you, and if she asks you to do anything in a lovely way, you never say…. NO…. about anything. Despite the fact that, at that time, you are worried about how much money you have.

Even though, if you have enough money then you will not worry about how much money you have to spend. You want to spend all the money for her happiness, for her to create good memories. You forget all things and you remember only one thing, how to spend some more and more time with her to deal with any expensive excuse. Same situation, I was in.)

We started finding an ATM. We saw an ATM and went there for withdrawing but the ATM was out of service. We went to another ATM and again went another ATM but they were cash less.

Then I asked a person, "Brother, do you know any ATM around here? Please tell me."

He pointed out, "There," the same ATM.

I said, "Brother, it's not working, we have just come from there. Do you know another somewhere and that's close to here?"

The person said, "Yes, there one."

I asked, "How to go and how far it is."

The person said, "It takes more than 15 minutes but there is also an ATM close to Cinema Hall."

We said, "Thank you so much, brother."

I smiled, looked at Anandita, and said to her, "I have an idea."

Anandita smiled and said, "Yes, I also have an idea and I think we have the same idea."

Then we told together each other with enthusiasms, "Why don't we go to Cinema Hall for watching movie…!"

I said, "But….!"

She asked, "But…What…?"

I said, "I mean, are you comfortable with me…?"

I didn't know, what was her opinion about me?

But she started laughing and replied, "Don't behave like a crazy… and don't go on my face. I'm a very dangerous girl."

I looked at her and smiled and said, "Oh…really….!"

She said, "Yes…so, don't worry about me and let's go."

Actually, our class was over about 4 pm and we spend more than one and half hour in restaurant and did some other things, and also in finding ATM. So we went very late to arrive at the Cinema Hall and it was about 7PM.

After arriving we went to Ticket counter and asked about the next show.

The person said, "One show is already going on. But another show will start at 09pm to 11:30pm."

We went to upset and said, "Oh no…!"

First I asked to Anandita, "Now tell me, what should we do now…? Because if we watch the next show. We will be too late to go back to the Hostel."

She said with sadly, "As you like."

I said, "You don't worry, if we've come here and decided to watch a movie, so you don't worry. We will definitely watch this movie."

I added, "Do you know what…? This is my favourite movie and I was waiting for a very long time, because I also have read a Novel, who has written already on this movie which is very interesting and full of romance, and I love to read the Novel, those are written by him. So, I have an idea, we will watch movie at any cost."

She asked me, "How…?"

I told her, "Okay, listen… first…. you make a call at your Hostel and say to them, today I can't come because I have come to my relative's place."

Anandita happily agreed with my idea, became very happy and asked me if it would be right whatever we had decided.

I said, "If we want to watch then we have to take this risk."

Anandita said, "Okay...!" and she did whatever I said, and I also did the same thing.

Thereafter, we took tickets and I said to her, "Now we have one and half hours. So let's go somewhere for spending our time?"

She said, "Okay..! Then let's go."

Thereafter, we started walking along the road.

When we were walking on the road, silently walking and kept walking;

Sometimes, she looked at me.

Sometimes, I looked at her.

Sometimes, we looked at each other, and smiled to look at each other.

Sometimes, somewhere....and so on.

I didn't understand what to talk about and the night journey was getting very boring.

I wanted to ask something. She also wanted to say something perhaps and tried to say but wasn't able to say and only smiled, then kept going.

At the end she couldn't stay silent. Anandita started asking with a smile, "Siddhu....!"

I replied with a surprise, "Yes......!"

She asked, "What's your dream…?"

I smiled and said, "My dream…, first of all…I want to be a Software Engineer, thereafter, about five to six years will do a job in any good company for getting good experience and for learning all things, as well as earn handsome money so that I can start my own business."

Anandita said, "Woo…impressive…!"

I asked, "Yes… and you, I mean…what's your dream..?"

Anandita smiled for a while and replied, "I don't know but now I have only one that I will get admission in good Engineering College first. Thereafter, I will see."

I smiled and said, "Thereafter…what…?"

Anandita said, "Of course, I mean…., I will study in Engineering college and after that will do a good job."

I laughed and said, "I thought that after Engineering, you will get married."

Anandita slapped me on my shoulder and replied, "What…? No…I mean…not after…after one and two years will do."

I said, "But I think…, after Engineering, very soon, I will get married in the first or two year of my job."

She said, "Okay but why…very soon….!"

I smiled and replied, "Actually, I want to experience both journey together….married life and working life."

She said, "Wow! That's a great idea…!"

I smiled and replied, "However, I know that both lives are very challenging, not easy to live."

She said, "Yes...okay, tell me one thing, how should your wife be? Have you ever thought...?"

I said, "What do you mean...?"

"I mean...as you know that everybody thinks and builds a beautiful dream about future life partner like I want this kind of wife who has these types of qualities like looking beautiful, educated, either housewife or doing job and so on but what is your opinion", She replied.

I said, "I never think like that but yes, I think that one thing must have...I mean, she must care about not only for me but also for my family members. I will also care and love her a lot and she will also. She must convince and stop me when I go at a wrong path, support me every moment. But I don't think it will happen."

She said, "Wow! It's really a great thinking and I pray to god that it happens to."

I said, "Thanks a lot and thank you very much but anyway tell me about you. What do you expect from your life partner...? I mean the same question if I ask."

Anandita smiled and answered, "First I want to do love marriage and the guy should respect me and care a lot like my father. I don't want that I come in his multiple choice options. I want that I'm his only one option."

I smiled and said, "Wow..! That's great thinking...!"

She smiled and said, "Yeah....! Thank you, but do you know what..? When my father is with me, I feel too much secure. When I told my father that Papa...I want to do this and that, and when I take any kind of decision, if that decision is wrong then he always tries to explain to me politely, why my decision was wrong for me; He never gets angry on me. He never forces me to do this and that. He always supports me at every moment."

I kept listening; thereafter I said, "Yes, it is absolutely right, and not only you but also every girl the same kind of thinking."

She said again, "When I get same feeling with the boy that I can secure with him thereafter at the any cost, I will get married with him."

I started laughing and said, "When you want to get married then you have to tell me, I will help you to find the boy."

She smiled and replied, "Sure…, but tell me, what is the time now…?"

I replied, "Oh no…! It's about 8:30PM, let's hurry up…!"

She said, "Okay…but I don't know one and half hour how has passed."

She added, "Do you know…what? Before, I was thinking what to do and how to spend that huge one and half hour but it has really gone. And I don't know how it is…? It's great moment for me."

I looked with enthusiasm and replied, "Yes, actually you are saying right. That was the great moment and today I'm so happy because first time I've been spending my time with a beautiful girl. I am lucky and this day is also lucky for me."

She said with laughing, "Oh….Really…!"

I smiled and said, "Yes...!"

She relied with cute smile, "Don't get smart. Let's hurry up…!"

I said, "Really, and thanks a lot for your trust on me because you are with me alone in the night."

She looked at me and smiled, after a while said, "Okay now let's go fast. We don't have enough time. Remember, if I miss any scenes of the movie then I will scratch your face and make you unlucky again." And she was laughing.

I said, "Okay let's go fast."

We ran fast and entered in the cinema hall. Sorry guys for, I didn't tell you the movie's name before. Actually; the movie name was "**Half Girl Friend**" and is written by **Chetan Bhagat**. We watched the movie and after watching we thought to watch the next show because we had no options to go back our Hostel but when we asked at the ticket counter about the next movie, they said, "No sir this is the last show."

Chapter-2

Terrible Night with Her

AT the time, it was 12AM. We were completely scared as to where to go at that time of night and how to go. We didn't know anybody in that town. There was very peaceful moment somewhere very dark while somewhere very light but some vehicles were going on.

I said to her, "I'm so scared…about…where and how to go now."

Suddenly she held my hand and looked at me, thereafter, I felt some courage. I smiled and told her thank you and we started laughing.

I told to her, "Now we have to search some safe place for spending whole night."

Anandita said, "Sidhu…! As you like but hurry up because I don't think, this is the good place for us. That's why I'm feeling scared and hungry also. So please…!"

I told her, "Me too."

I said, "But dear…! Don't worry. I'm with you and you don't need to feel scared with me."

I held her hand tightly and asked, "How are you feeling now…?"

She stated laughing and said, "Now I'm feeling great."

I also started laughing and said, "I think. We should have to find and to go to railway station, or any temple for spending whole night but if we go to railway station then we can take some food because we are also feeling very hungry."

She said, "Yes, that's a good idea."

After long time, Anandita saw that a vehicle was coming then she said, "Sidhu…! I think, a vehicle is coming, may be, it's an auto, wave your hand to stop."

I waved my hand an auto. The auto driver stopped his auto and asked us, "Sir…! Where do you want to go?"

Firstly, we looked into the auto there was empty. Thereafter we looked to each other.

The auto driver said, "Sir…! What are you thinking this is my last trip. Sir…! Don't think enough please and hurry up…! I'm going late."

I asked him, "Uncle…! We want to go to railway station. So how much distance from here and how much fair do you take?"

The driver said, "Sir…! It is about 5 km and its fare is only 20 rupees per person."

I looked at her asked, "What do you say…we should sit or not…?"

She said, "I think, we should go because we don't have any another option."

I told to the driver, "Uncle! Please don't mind but may I take a pic of your auto number?"

The driver said, "It's okay, Sir! But please do hurry up!"

After taking a pic we went to sit into the auto and he started riding. She send an auto pic to her close friend and wrote, "My dear friend this is an auto number. Please call me tomorrow morning. If I receive your call then It's Okay but if not then please you help me and my friend…Siddhartha for finding." and same thing I did.

In the way, I asked him, "Uncle! Do you know any restaurant near to railway station for taking dinner?"

He said, "Yes, there are many but now all of them have closed now."

I said, "Okay! Don't worry, let's go quickly!"

He said again, "Sir there is a place where a restaurant available and keep opening 24 hours but the place is not good for both of you. If you don't mind you are like my children. So would you like to come to my home? And if you want to spend night at my home then you can."

Suddenly, some doubt arose in my mind. She held my hand tightly and with her scared face she looked at me and tried to tell me and her eyes was saying indirectly, "Please say him no!"

I understood. Anandita was trying to tell me, to say him no, from the way of the holding my hand and her eyes activities.

I said, "Don't worry…uncle! We will manage."

He said, "Okay! Are you sure and you will manage…?"

We said together, "Yes uncle….! You don't worry….!"

On the way, at the roadside, suddenly, the driver stopped the auto and said, "Please wait here, my home is very nearby. So I just come within 10 minutes."

I asked him, "Where are you going?"

The driver replied, "Don't need to get scared...my dear children, I will just come back."

There was a street that was not very wide. And he entered in the street.

When the driver went, she trembled with fear and said, "What happens to him now... and why is he going....?"

I cuddled her and said, "Anandita.... listen to me dear...!"

She said, "Sidhu! I'm so scared now."

I said, "Dear.... don't worry! Nothing will happen. I am with you and I think he is a nice person and because of some important reason he is going to his home, so we should trust him."

Actually, when I saw her condition, I was scared too but she was more than me. If I told her that I was also scared, then what would happen I didn't know. That's why I was not telling her that I was scared too. We kept sitting in the Auto.

After some time, I told her to sit properly. I asked her, "Do you have pencil or pen....?"

Anandita asked to me, "Why do you need now...?"

I said, "Put out from your bag first....!"

She said, "Okay....!" And she put out a pen and told me to take it.

I smiled and said, "Don't give me, put it in your pocket and we don't need to scare now, this is our tool."

She said, "You are scaring me...?"

I laughed and said, "Not at all, we just need to be active."

I added, "You laugh now."

She asked with a puzzled look, "But…why…now…?"

I smiled and replied, "If you laugh, then your fear will go."

She smiled and kept her head on my shoulder and I said, "We are our strengths."

Then she said, "I have a Compass also, so can I take it out…?"

I smiled and said, "Yes ma'am….please….!"

Thereafter, we were very active with our tools.

She asked me again and again to build her cute lovely face with sweet voice just like a little child and said, "When he will come back."

I started smiling when I looked her face.

Again she asked same things again and again, "When he will come back…please tell me?"

And I was just looking her and smiling then she started beating, thereafter, I said, "Don't be scared and I'm with you. He told us to come very soon."

Similarly, we were waiting and I had full water bottle in my bag. We kept waiting and sometimes I starting drinking water and sometimes she drank but without feeling thirsty.

Almost 15 minutes had passed but every minute was taking almost 1 hour for us.

Without feeling thirsty, when I drank full bottle after some time I started feeling to pee.

I said to her, "May I go just for two minutes."

She asked, "Please you don't go anywhere and leave me alone here."

I laughed and said, "Dear, please try to understand. It's an emergency (for passing pee) and I can't control now."

She understood and said, "Me too, from long time, I am trying to control it but I was feeling shy to tell you and when you told me so I too."

I began to laugh and said, "It's okay, it happens."

She said, "So what happened?"

I smiled and said, "Nothing….first you go and I will go after you."

She said, "No, I can't go alone please you also come with me. Just look outside, it's very dark place. So please…!"

I said, "No, no, I can't come with you. Are you mad and how can I come with you…?"

She said, "Listen, I agree to do it in my pant but I can't go in the dark night alone. And I have never gone alone before."

I said, "What a crazy girl you are…?"

She replied, "Yes! I am."

I said, "Okay, you don't worry. When we reach railway station then there must have a Toilet Flat. We will do it there."

Anandita said, "Please-please dear now please try to understand I can't control now. It is out of my control."

I said, "You are totally mad girl. Okay let's go."

At the time, it was around 1AM and that was a very dark night. I told her to come with me. We went together and I stopped after going some distance and said to her, "Now…you don't need to be scared. I stay here and you can go."

Anandita said, "Okay..., but stay here, you don't go anywhere until I come back."

"You don't worry," I said.

Anandita went some distance and I turned back. After a few moments later, my naughty mind starting creating and I felt like playing a horrible prank on her.

I just said, "Oh my god....! What is standing there?"

She began to cry loudly and said, "Mammy-Mammy...! Where is...?"

I started laughing and said, "I'm so sorry...sorry...! Nothing is there. I was just kidding."

Anandita said, "If you joke like that again then I'll come as I am now."

I said again, "Okay-okay-okay...just relax...! I'm really-really very sorry, please do fast. I think, the driver has come because someone is standing there. He must be there."

She came quickly and started beating me hard on my back four-five times with her hand and said, "What was...?"

I started laughing and said, "I'm sorry-sorry...!" and ran fast from there.

She said, "Where are you going...stay here? I bring out your stupid jokes in you."

I ran away from there and went another way. She also came running after me.

The auto driver said, "Sir, where are you going, please come soon."

I told her, "Listen..., he is calling us, if he goes then I don't know where to go. So please try to understand."

She said, "Okay…, come and let's go."

I said, "You promise me, don't hit me again."

She said, "Okay…, now come, I don't…."

I told her, "You go, I will come soon."

She asked me, "why…?"

I said, "Yaar…! I'm also in an emergency situation. So please try to understand."

She started laughing and said, "May I stay here? May be, you will get scared too like me."

And she started coming towards me.

I said, "No-no-no and never please.., I don't need your help please you go…!"

She said, "Okay, but tell me one thing…whatever you did, if I came in the same way. Then…?"

I said, "Listen…, believe me, I didn't see anything and now I apologise to you my dear mother (Kaali Maa). Please go now…!"

I bowed my head and apologized to her. She started smiling, looking at my face and said, "Okay…., my dear son. Now you can do your emergency work."

Thereafter, she went back to the Auto and I took a deep breath. I quickly finished off my emergency work and reached there.

The driver asked us, "Where had you gone?"

I said, "Nothing uncle it was some emergency situation but where had you gone and also came so late?"

The driver said, "I'm sorry, actually I went to my home. It is very close from here but when I asked you to come to my home for dinner, you refused to come and I also saw her scared face in my mirror. So I understood that you were scared of me. That's why I have brought some dishes for you. Please have it. And that's why I came late."

I smiled and said, "Uncle, actually this is totally unknown place for us and that's why. I'm sorry about it."

She also said, "Yes uncle that's the matter and you are also unknown for us. So how can I take? That's why."

The driver said, "Okay! I understand and that's good. Now let's go." We quickly got into the Auto and the driver started driving.

When we were going to the station, we saw a big function on the way. Some singer was singing a song, everybody was dancing. I also wanted to go there.

I asked the driver, "Listen uncle! How much time it will take to reach the station from here?"

He said, "Not enough, we are just about to reach within 5 minutes."

And when we arrived at the Railway Station, we looked around. We saw there were many people sleeping there.

I asked her, "What do you say? Do you want to stay here?"

She was looking very happy and said, "I thing, we should go to visit the function. Because I don't feel good to stay here, just look at this place. What do you say…? "

I said, "Exactly that's a great idea and I also wanted to tell you the same."

"Okay, then let's go", she said.

We went there and saw there was fast food also available. She said, "let's go and eat first because I'm too hungry."

Then I told Anandita to sit on a bench and I went to order. We ordered two plates of Pav-bhaji in the same plate, after finishing it, we also ate what the Auto driver had brought for us.

When we felt that our stomach was full, we went to see the function and saw every person was enjoying and dancing.

She told me that she wanted to go dancing because she told me she loved to dance.

And I said to her, "Then why are we waiting? Let's go but I'm sorry, I can't and I don't know how to dance."

She told me, "My dear friend, I don't know too. But let's enjoy the moment and come on, just do it."

She again said, "Don't think about others, just think only you and me are there."

I felt confident after hearing her words.

Actually, I knew dancing but not so well and I just used to dance like they dance in a village marriage. We went in the function. Anandita was very excited to dance and very soon started dancing but I was feeling uncomfortable to dance in front of her. When she told me to dance then I started dancing slowly-slowly. That was the first time I was dancing with a girl.

Gradually, we started enjoying the moments and without thinking about others, stared dancing just like that day was my last day. Many people stopped their dancing and stood around us and started seeing us dance.

At 5 o'clock the program finished. We went to the railway station. We had tea and bread there.

Thereafter, I dropped her at her Hostel and I also went to my Hostel.

Chapter-3

Birth of a Beautiful Friendship

That day our class was at 12:00pm. We entered the class. I seemed everybody got to know about us. That's why when we entered the class, everybody started asking about the last night.

At lunch time my friends started asking me and her friends asked her about the night, "So what happened last night and why did you send me the message."

Then we told them whole story about last night.

Anandita also told Pallavi and Manu about me. Actually, Pallavi was Manu's friend.

Anandita told her, "Do you know…what…? He is very nice boy but a little shy, a little naughty and a little idiot but I don't know how, I have just started loving him."

Pallavi said to Anandita, "What about him…I mean…Siddhartha loves you or not…?"

Anandita replied, "No…he doesn't love me but I love him because when I was with him, every time, whole night, I felt safe and good with him."

Anandita said to them, "But I don't know and why….? and now tell me one thing, when you meet a person for the first time after the first meeting, you are ready to go with him anywhere like... in the night for doing fun, watching movie, dancing and so on."

Manu replied, "Of course not, after first meeting I can't go even with a girl at night, forget a boy."

Anandita interrupted with enthusiasm and replied, "Exactly, but I went and I don't know...why I was spend with him whole night. When he told me go then I got ready to go. But no one questions were appeared in my mind about him like...how is his nature, go with him it would safe for me or not?"

Pallavi said, "Okay! Just leave it, first you have to know whether he loves you or not."

Anandita got sad and said, "I know he doesn't love me because he likes someone else."

Pallavi and Manu asked with excitement, "Who is the girl...?"

Anandita started looking towards Manu and said, "You...!"

Manu wonderfully said, "What...is he crazy?"

Anandita said, "Yes...it's right. He really loves you."

Pallavi started laughing and said, "Mamta...I know that he likes you. But you don't believe."

Anandita became doubtful and asked, "Please tell me all things that what was happened?"

Then Pallavi told Anandita all things about me and whatever happened."

Anandita said, "These things, he never told me before; Okay I will ask him."

Pallavi and Manu told Anandita everything, but when they were narrating all things, their way of saying was not good, it was as if they were making fun of me.

When the class was over Anandita called me and told me to wait for her. I started waiting for her. She came after a while and said, "Let's go."

So we were going together towards her Hostel, and she asked me, "Doggy… you never said before about Mamta that you have already talked to her."

I asked, "Who said…?"

Anandita replied, "None of your business."

I said, "Okay…, but I know that either Manu or Pallavi had said this to you. That's why they were smiling after seeing me."

Anandita said, "Exactly…and what do you think if you don't tell me then I wouldn't keep know..?"

I asked, "It's not like that. I didn't feel good to share with these things, therefore, I ignored to tell you and anyway…what did they tell you…?"

Anandita said, "Nothing…only…when I told them about last night they shared with me about you and whatever you did."

I said, "You told them only about the last night's story or something else…?"

Anandita lied to me because she is a girl and she knew very well how a girl behaves. That's why she told me a lie and didn't tell me that they had spoken jokingly which I felt very sad to hear. Thereafter I started feeling embarrassed in front of them.

So she normally said, "No...I said only these things and nothing else but we have to know first, Mamta has boyfriend or not....?"

Anandita said that she was trying to know that Mamta had boyfriend. I requested Anandita to ask her friend "Pallavi" whether Manu has a boyfriend or not...?.

Before that night, we were just friends but after that night we became more than friends. From the day, she kept my new nick name and kept calling me 'Doggy' and I kept calling her new nick name 'Jangli-billi'.

She cared for me a lot. Whenever I felt sad without saying anything, she knew and realized that something was going wrong with me then she cared for me just like a mother caring and helped me in every situation.

Sometimes, she fought for me against anybody if anybody tried to disturb me. Every time, she tried to be happy.

Every time she asked me, "What did you eat, what you are doing, and so on."

She was totally mad but she became my best friend and a favourite for me.

I also didn't live without talking to her.

One day, I was in hostel and Anandita phoned and asked me, "What you are doing Doggy?

I said, "Nothing, just lying on the bed."

She asked again, "Why..., are you well...any problem...?"

I said, "Yes! I'm good."

She replied, "Okay, but you sound like…you are not good, so what did you eat today…?"

I just told to her, "Today I'm too hungry because of the Hostel dishes, these were too bad, didn't like to eat what was given to me."

Anandita asked, "So what happen, did you eat anything or not…?"

I said, "No, I ate just a little but I didn't feel like eating more."

She said, "Okay just wait…!"

I thought that she went somewhere for doing her work, thereafter, I also started doing my study.

"(At the time, I think, it was month of June and that was a very hot day and the day was Sunday, people were afraid to go outside because it was too much hot. Where I was living in the Hostel, there were no any vehicles available to come towards my Hostel. I used to walk about one Kilometres and reach on the main road where I took an auto to go to her Hostel and anywhere. One day she came with me to see my Hostel where I was living. So she knew how to come to my Hostel.)"

About, after half an hour she phoned me to come outside to the Hostel.

I asked her, "Why and where are you…now…?"

Anandita said, "I don't know. Shut your mouth and just come outside right now…idiot…!"

When I came outside, I was surprised to see. Actually, she was standing outside my Hostel. When I went to her, she put out something from her bag and said, "Now you go and eat it."

I said, "Wha-wha-what? Are you mad? What was the need it…?"

I-I-I didn't know and I was totally shocked. What to say to her. I kept smiling and kept looking at her. I seemed just like about to cry.

And at that time, she was also smiling at me. I felt like tightly hugging her but it was not possible there.

Anandita said, "Doggy… now don't do much drama. Go and eat it."

I gave her the dish which she brought for me and said, "Put it in your bag, and wait and stand here, I will just come."

Anandita said, "For what…? I need to go."

I said, "Stay here…I will come back very soon…!"

Anandita smiled and said, "Okay…come back soon…!"

I went into my Hostel and quickly got ready and took my wallet and umbrella, came outside and said to her, "let's go somewhere."

"But where…?" said Anandita.

"Don't know," said I.

We went to a restaurant and packed some more items and took a water bottle, went near a park where we sat under a tree and opened all items and said, "Now open your mouth and eat this morsel."

At first she refused to take a single morsel and said, "No I can't because I have brought for you, not for me, because you are hungry, not me, and you told me that you are hungry."

Anandita snatched the dish from my hand and took one morsel and said, "You take it first, otherwise I will slap below your ear and you will see stars in the daytime."

I started laughing and said, "Okay you feed me and I will feed you."

Anandita said, "Okay but not enough because I just ate."

(But actually, Anandita had not eaten before coming because when she came and stood near my Hostel and told me to come outside and when I was coming out to my Hostel that why she was telling me to come out side, I want to know that what was the matter?. At that time, her friend who was living with her in the Hostel, called me and said, "Siddhartha.....I don't know what happened to Anandita. We were about to eat but at that time Anandita talked with someone and suddenly she told me that she needed to go somewhere and would come back and eat. Thereafter, she got ready quickly and had gone somewhere, and I don't where...she has gone...?"

Her friend said again, "I called her many times for asking her what happened but she was not receiving my calls now."

I said to Anandita's friend, "Okay, don't worry. She is just crazy and now she is standing outside my Hostel and calling me just now. So please don't worry, I will call you later and take care," and I disconnected the call.)

Thereafter, Anandita fed me and I fed her. While doing so, we finished the entire meal and we spend some more time there till late evening. Then I dropped her near her Hostel and I came back to my Hostel.

Sometimes Anandita came to sit next to me when the seat was empty and sometimes she sat with Pallavi.

Due to regular talk, Anandita became Pallavi's good friend.

When Anandita was with me, sometimes she behaved like a little cute child and sometimes troubled me and sometimes to something else.

I really started loving her company and I used to get a lot of pleasure from her naughty activities. But sometime I became angry if she behaved more like this, then she would stop from doing such behaviour and she held her ears and say, "Sorry...sorry...sorry....!"

She would keep repeating until I smiled and said, "It's okay...don't worry...!", then she would hug me.

But she fought with anybody for me and cared me a lot.

I noticed for a very long time that Manu was again not coming. When I was in class, my eyes were always looking for her.

Thereafter, one day I said to Anandita to ask Pallavi about Manu, why didn't she come...?

Then Anandita asked to Pallavi about Manu, "Why didn't she come...?"

Pallavi said to Anandita, "I don't know. Why...? But she told me that she is leaving this institute and the Hostel too."

Then Anandita shared the information with me and told me to forget Manu because she has left the institute. When I got to know that she has left the institution I became so sad and asked her, "But why..?"

Anandita said, "I don't know. I asked her friend. But she didn't say any reason to me. May be, she also doesn't know."

I told Anandita in a calm voice, "Okay....just leave it and forget her (Manu)" but I knew very well that it was not possible for me to forget her easily and really that was not easy for me to forget her as soon as.

Every day I got ready with full energy for going to class but I used to be very sad when I entered the class and got to know that she was again not present in the class. My eyes were always waiting for her and used to search her, and kept searching her with expectations that one day she might come. My ears were always longing to hear her beautiful voice, were missing her laughter.

It became my habit to look for her after entering the class. After I did not see her, I became upset and didn't study well and my whole day used to go in a worst manner.

Not only that, whenever someone entered into the class, I would see with complete joy that Manu would probably come now but if she was not then I used to get sad again.

At the beginning, Manu was coming regular to attend the class but suddenly she stopped coming. After her leaving the institute, I felt like, I was building a house for years with hopes and expectations, decorating my dreams and my dreams were about to be fulfilled but suddenly an earthquake came and it shattered all the dreams, all hopes, and all expectations. It made me completely homeless, hopeless, and dreamless.

When Anandita saw me unhappy and that I didn't study like before. She came to ask me the reason of my unhappiness but I refused to tell anything and said, "Nothing...happen...!"

But Anandita got to know my feelings. She easily read my face that I was happy or unhappy, she was my best friend and because of my unhappiness, she was always worried about me and cared for me a lot.

Anandita couldn't stay without knowing, the reason for my sadness and she asked to me again and again, "What happen, Doggy…! I am seeing you for some days; you are looking very sad and don't study and talk like before."

I smiled and replied in a refusing way and said, "Nothing…happen…Jangli-Billi, it's okay. I'm good."

She said, "Are you sure….?"

I said, "Yes….I'm sure….!"

But really I missed her a lot. Sometime I used to pray to God, somehow make me see her once. I was sad because of Manu. But how could I say to Anandita that I missed Manu so much?

I felt embarrassing to tell her. But Anandita understood and came to know that I was missing her.

One day, when the class was finished, we were returning to our Hostel together. Anandita held my hand and told me to come and let's go somewhere.

I went along her and asked to her, "What happen…?"

She replied, "Nothing! I just need to know something about you. So just keep quiet and come with me."

Thereafter, she took me in a park. We found a good place and sat.

Anandita looked at me angrily and she was confused that how to start and ask?

I laughed and asked, "What happen now…any problem…?"

She replied, "Look...! I know very well that you are always missing Manu. If you consider me your best friend, then why are you not even telling...?

Look...., I can read your face and get to know all things so you can't hide anything from me."

I laughed and said, "No-no...it's like that, I told you that I'm okay."

Anandita said, "Dude...just stop laughing...!" And she got sad, looked down and again said, "Okay....I should have to understand. I even share my private matters when happens to me, what date it happens to me, you get to know before me."

I just smiled and said, "Yes....so what...?"

Anandita looked me and said, "Nothing...so what...! Do you remember...? One day...you called me at 10 o'clock in the night but I told you that my stomach was hurting and I couldn't be able to talk now. So you hung up the phone after saying take-care."

I said, "Yes...so...what...I just felt that you might have this problem and it's my intuition...nothing else...!"

Anandita added, "Of course! I can understand but I thought that you have gone to sleep but after a while you called me and told me to come outside near the gate and you gave me Pad with some medicines too."

I smiled and said, "Yes...! Mad girl! Why are you telling now...?"

But Anandita didn't smile and said, "You are mad and I'm telling you because really I wanted to tell you at that time, I don't have Pad and I also went to the nearest shop but it was not open, and I didn't have enough courage to go somewhere because of intense pain, and before your calling, I wanted to call you and tell you to bring a 'PAD' for me. So I took my phone and dialled your number several times and wanted to call you but didn't have courage to call and I felt embarrassing to tell you. Because of which I used a cloth."

She was just speaking and kept speaking then I laughed and interrupted and said, "Okay-okay…I'm understanding. So just relax and first drink water." And I passed the water bottle.

She refused to drink water and kept telling, "When you came with 'PAD' and medicines, I was shocked to see, and also very happy, at that time and before, I was using only Pad. I didn't know that there were medicines also available for that and I didn't ever try to them."

I was just smiling and listening carefully and kept saying….Yes….and…No…..!

Again Anandita said, "You know that I'm from the village side. I'm alone and I didn't tell all this to anyone except my mother but not so much in detail and not even to my father, and not even to friends (girls) easily. But now I share and tell you because I feel safe with you but do not feel suffocated with you."

She added more, "It is very difficult to find good friends in this unknown city. I thought that without saying you got to know girl's problem and understood my problem; that was enough for me and that's why I consider you to be my best friend. When I tell you anything either happiness or sadness, you listen with great love. I would feel very pleasure by telling you a small thing. Till…I don't tell, it seems like something that I'm missing. I'm telling you all this because I believe in you and trust you."

I just kept smiling and looking at her sometimes also feeling bored but Anandita was saying so it was okay for me and thought that since when did I become so much important for her…..?

Anandita smiled and asked, "What happen…? Stop smiling…idiot…!"

I smiled and said, "Nothing! Keep talking…I'm listening."

Anandita said, "You are smiling, but believe me when you came first time and gave me the Pad and some medicines, you wouldn't believe me how much happy I was. I felt like hugging you but I couldn't do."

I said, "So what's the delay now you can do it….!"

Then Anandita smiled and said, "Why not….?"

And she hugged me for some moments and started crying and she said, "Now you promise me that you will share everything with me and never leave me alone."

I smiled and said, "Yes…Jangli-Billi…I will do, now happy…!" then I called a person who was selling popcorn. He came and gave me popcorn and I gave him money and said to him, "Brother just look at her she is crying."

He asked the reason of crying. I said, "Nothing…her boyfriend left her that's why."

Anandita started beating me and said to him, "No brother, he is telling a lie." Thereafter, I cuddled her for a while.

The person was about 25 years old, also began to take interest a little more. He smiled and said, "Okay…don't cry and make him your boyfriend," and pointed towards me.

I said, "Yes...brother...I will think but now you can go."

He smiled and went to say...okay brother...!

We started eating popcorn. I looked at her with a smile then she looked at me as I wanted to say her something and she looked and was waiting to hear.

I smiled and became busy to eating popcorn again. She kept looking angrily and said, "Eat this too, gourmet," throwing another popcorn packet towards me.

Then I smiled and said, "Okay-okay...I'm sorry...!"

When I told, she got ready to hear just like I wanted to say something again. But I said, "Okay-okay...I'm sorry...I will not be able to eat completely. You also eat something."

And I began to feed her with my own hand. But she refused to take and threw it.

I used to call her a Jangli-Billi, that was true because when she got angry, she exactly looked like a Jangli-Billi.

So, I said, "I keep calling you Jangli-Billi, I'm absolutely right because when you are angry, you really look the same."

Anandita showed her tongue and said, "You look like a Doggy...!" with anger.

I said, "Okay-Okay...just relax...what I tell you, you know very well but if you want to hear from my side then listen...yes...I love her, and after her absence. My eyes were always waiting for her and I missed her a lot but I know that she will not come again then what's the point of missing."

I said again, "Yes! I'm missing her always, I will forget and try to forget her but it's not possible for me to suddenly forget her. It takes some time. But I say thanks to God that he gave me a best friend like you. Really! I'm very happy and feeling very pleasure when you are with me"

I smiled and added, "My dear….Jangli-Billi… I consider myself very lucky because you are with me."

Thereafter, I looked her smiling face and she smiled and said, "Hay…..my dear Doggy…my child..! Now…come! Let me love you." And she hugged me.

After sometime, she said, "Now let's go to hostel."

So I dropped her near her hostel and I came back to my hostel. When I arrived to my hostel, I called her and told her that I arrived because after arriving, we called and inform each other that we reached safely. That was our friendship and way of caring.

After dinner I called her again and made fun of her by saying, "Jangli-Billi…you said all that no one has said till date. Since when did all this happen…love me so much…don't you…?"

Anandita said, "Doggy…don't fly too much…be a Doggy, stay like a pet and my lovely dog. What have you done for a little love, now don't pee to climb on the shoulder."

Similarly, while arguing, we fell asleep wishing each other 'good night'. It was not a matter of one day. We used to have good nights like that every day.

Chapter-4

Expectations, Wishes and the Beautiful Gift

One day when I was returning to my class, (That day Anandita hadn't gone for some reason.) It was about 8 pm and Anandita called me. I pulled out my phone from my pocked and received her call.

Anandita said cheerfully, "Doggy…! Where are you…?"

I replied, "I'm outside and going to my hostel. What happened?"

Anandita said, "Nothing….don't cancel the call and hold on….!"

I was totally unknown about what was happening and I asked her but she said, "Just hold on…, there is a surprise for you." and she started calling someone.

Actually Anandita called Pallavi and Anandita told her to call her.

I was in doubt and asked, "What is going on….will you please tell me…?"

Anandita said, "Why do you talk a lot….Doggy……!" and she said, "Just keep quite…and wait…!"

And Pallavi started calling someone again.

I was on conference call with someone and Anandita said, "Doggy...now talk to your special person and this is a surprise for you."

I said, "Hello...! Hello...! Hello...!" nobody was speaking only laughing.

I asked to Anandita, "Jangli...who is she, without saying anything only, why is laughing...?"

Anandita also laughed and said, "Recognise her, who is she...?"

I was trying to recognise the voice that was laughing. But I couldn't then I asked her, "Who are you...?"

Anandita said to me, "Doggy...you don't know her."

I said, "No...! Really....! Not enough. But it seems like this laughing sounds familiar to me if I'm not wrong is it Manu...?"

That third person, that was a girl and said, "Hello....! You didn't recognise me. It's me Mamta."

I said, "Waooo....great to meet you...! But you are only Manu for me and how can I forget you."

At the time, I felt like my breathing has stopped and I was totally shocked, then I took a few deep breaths and thought that how it had been possible.

Of course, because of Anandita, my dear lovely friend and...! My all and everything happened because of Anandita.

I said to Anandita, "Thank you so much my dear and my lovely Jangli-Billi.

Manu said, "What's this...Anandita call you Doggy and you call her Jangli-Billi."

Pallavi laughed and said to Manu, "Mamta...Both of them are like this...you just see."

Manu (Mamta) said, "Oh....great....friendship...!"

Anandita laughed and I said to Anandita, "I don't know you would even do like that but really...today I'm so happy and thank you, thank you so much again and again my lovely angel and Jangli-Billi. If you have been in front of me right now, I would give you a cute hug."

Manu interrupted and said, "I also want your cute hug," And was laughing

Thereafter, Anandita interrupted and told Manu, "Hey...! He speaks like that but you don't worry, you talk to him and he is totally crazy about you and wanted to talk. That's why I did this."

I said to Manu, "No...Manu...it's not like that and she is lying like this. That's why I call her Jangli-Billi."

Manu started laughing and said to Anandita, "Anandita...look! What he's saying?"

Anandita said to Manu, "He is Doggy that's why he is behaving like this." And said, "Manu...now you both talk."

Manu asked to Anandita, "Now...where are you going...?"

Anandita said, "I just come...you talk to him because he was cray to talk to you."

Manu said, "Hello...Siddhartha....!"

I started talking to Manu and said, "Hello....! How are you....?"

Manu replied, "I'm good and you...?"

I said, "Me too…! It's a pleasure to meet you and really I had lost my hope that you will meet me again but today it's happened."

Manu told me, "I also feel good to talk to you and my friend…Pallavi and Anandita told me, about you that you wanted to talk and like me too."

I laughed and said, "Yes…may be but what do you think…?"

Manu laughed and told me, "Okay…I don't know but they told me that's why I was sure because when I was coming in the class and by seeing your behaviour, it seemed that you liked me. And I also noticed you that you looked towards me again and again."

I laughed and said, "I think so…!"

Manu laughed and said, "You think so…? Then why didn't you tell me before. If you like me…?"

I only kept laughing and said, "I don't know…why…? But I was afraid about rejection, that's why."

Manu said again, "Actually…, remember the day…when you gave me to write something at your Notebook. I thought that you are a good boy but a little crazy. I also started liking you and wanted to talk to you and to be friends with you so that we can help each other in study but I didn't have courage to tell you. You were looking as if you have an arrogant personality and I thought that you should have to go on the Himalayas because you didn't speak more, didn't laugh and only did study."

My happiness knew no bounds, when I got to know that, Manu also liked me. She told me that I looked like a nice boy and very serious about studies. And she also said, "Really I started liking you, wanted to talk you and with you."

I became happy and asked, "Really...you wanted to talk to me and did you like me."

Manu said, "Yes...you can ask Pallavi...?"

Pallavi was also on conference then she said, "Yes...she started liking you. But after some days we saw your behaviour was totally changed, you were behaving very rude and aggressive."

I said, "No-No...! It's not like that, actually because of my study, I did. You can ask to Anandita. How my nature is..?"

Manu said to me, "Yes! I know everything, but I had some doubt. However, today my doubt have been totally clear by speaking with you."

I said, "Thank you so much. And do you know.... what...? I wanted and tried to tell you many time but I didn't."

Manu said, "But I knew that you liked me."

I laughed and asked, "Yes...but how do you know...?"

Manu said, "I just knew."

I said, "I think...Jangli has told you."

Manu laughed and said to me, "My dear, I also told you before that I liked your behaviour. It does not matter who told me."

I said, "Okay, I tried to talk and to tell you several times but I was afraid to think about my study. Because...., I didn't want to lose my opportunity again. That's why."

Again I said, "One day when the class was over then I followed you a little distance but suddenly I started feeling, it is not good to follow you, thereafter I came back and changed my way."

Manu said, "Oh...Really...!"

I said, "Yes...! It's true. But I noticed you, and I saw, sometimes a boy came to meet you and sometimes also sat beside you. So I thought that he was your boyfriend and if I shared you my feeling and if you replied that you were engaged somewhere it would have been embarrassing for me that I was thinking and really it was not good expectable for me. That's why I didn't want to even tell you."

Manu said, "No-no, he was not my boyfriend. He just knew me and nothing more. But after some days, I didn't know...why....your behaviour had changed? Because, when I talked and tried to ask you anything then you talked but replied to me every times very rudely and arrogantly. Suddenly, what happened with you and why did you do that...?"

I said, "Yes...., you're right...! Actually I wanted to ignore you and didn't want to see your face and your beautiful eyes. I've seen many girls beautiful than you but your face has become fixed in my mind. Because of it, it distracted me every time but when you didn't come, my eyes wanted to see you and it used to search you here and there. I didn't feel good at the day and used to get restless."

When I was talking to Manu, I didn't know how time passed. It was more than one hour and I was going to Hostel while talking but I didn't know where I was going and reached. Suddenly I saw the road was blocked, I mean, the road was ended.

I laughed and said to Manu, "Manu...while talking with you, I don't know, where I have come and the road has ended."

Manu started laughing and said, "Idiot...., first of all, what's Manu...it's not my name....dear, just call me Mamta and second thing...., Go back the same way."

I smiled and said, "I don't mind whatever your name, I love to call you Manu, that's why."

Anandita interrupted and said, "Yes...Manu! Oh... sorry... Mamta....! He always keeps repeating your name and every time, so it becomes my habit that's why, sometimes I also keep telling you...same name...Manu! Actually at the beginning, I told him that your name is Mamta, not Manu. So do you know...what... did he reply...? He said that he loves Manu that's why he keeps calling you Manu." And she laughed.

Manu laughed and said, "Anyway keep calling..., whatever you want, I don't mind."

And again said, "You've found out your right path or not....?"

I said, "Yes I'm trying."

Then I went back and came very soon on the right path and reached my Hostel.

I told her, "Manu......! Now I have reached my Hostel.

Manu said, "Okay now I have to go and now I'm ending the call."

I asked, "Why...?"

Manu replied, "Because if I keep talking with you some more then you will not sleep whole night and me too, that's why."

I asked, "But when will you come again because you are not coming for some days?"

Manu laughed and told me, "Now, I can't come."

I said with a sad tone, "Oooo...! But...., why....?

Manu said, "Because I'm getting married after a few months. I have some work there and when I come, I will definitely come to meet you dear."

I said, "What is the use of meeting me when you are getting married?"

Then Manu told me, "You don't worry, I will do something and now you go."

That day, when Manu told me that she was getting married. I became upset and I was about to cry. So I said to Manu, "Manu...please wait...!"

Manu asked, "Okay...tell...! Are you fine...?"

I controlled my tears and asked, "Yes, I'm fine. But Manu! Now tell me one thing...today I either cry or become happy. What to do...first....?"

Manu got doubtful and asked, "What do you mean...?"

I said, "I mean...I become happy because you met me after a long time and talked to me after a long time and you told me that one day you would come here to meet me.

Or I cry, because you will be getting married. So please tell me...what do I do first...? Be happy or cry..., please tell me..., what to do first...?"

I think at that time, Manu became totally confused and she didn't have any word for replying so she kept say, "Sorry…I'm not getting your points, what do you mean…?"

Anandita interrupted and said, "Manu! Just relax…will you please cut the call from your side right now? I will talk you later, please….!"

Manu hung up her phone and Anandita started convincing me and said, "Doggy! Are you crazy…? Firstly I don't know, whether she will be getting married or not and what's the purpose of telling…? But you don't need to be upset and I am with you."

I said, "Okay…you don't worry…I'm okay…!"

Anandita said, "Okay….first you get freshened up and after that call me and just relax. I'm with you."

Saying this she hung up her phone.

But at the last moment, when Manu was telling that she would do something, the needle of my watch got stuck on it I was totally confused.

So I entered my Hostel and threw my bag on my bed and again called Anandita. But she didn't pick up. She might be was busy somewhere, still I didn't understand that and I kept on calling again and again.

Anandita was in the washroom. When her friend saw that I kept calling again and again then her friend called Anandita and said, "Anandita…who is Doggy….he is calling you again and again…?"

When Anandita got to know I was calling several times then she replied inside the washroom, "Hay….Suhani….he is Siddhartha and tell him, I'm in the washroom and coming soon."

Suhani picked up and said the same thing. Then I told her to ask her to call me back as soon as possible.

Anandita quickly came out and called me back, "Yes...doggy tell me and I know that you threw your bag and started calling me. So tell me."

I said, "Just leave it and tell me one thing, as Manu said that she is about to get married but again she said that she would do something."

Anandita said, "I don't know but you don't think much that Manu will be getting married as she told you."

I said, "Yes I know and you are saying right that I don't need to think much about it."

Again I said, "Okay bye and good night, see you tomorrow."

I just told Anandita that I didn't need to think much about Manu and try to forget her. But it was not easy for me to forget her.

That night, I couldn't sleep well the whole night I was thinking about her and going to think-think and going to think and think again and again think, "Is it real that she is getting married or was she was just telling a lie? But anyway...think positive." I kept saying this to myself.

So I started thinking positive and the thinking was, "She is not getting married and if she was not then I will definitely get married to her."

Thereafter, I was trying to sleep many times but I couldn't.

When Manu was speaking with me on phone then she told me, "Now I'm cutting the call because if I keep talking to you some more then you will not get sleep whole night and me too."

I think Manu was telling me the truth, really...! I couldn't sleep whole night. Sometimes I went to sleep on bed and tried to sleep but when I closed my eyes to sleep, "Whatever Manu told me and those things of every moments were coming in my mind."

These moments didn't let me sleep well then I woke up and went to my study place and sometimes I was trying to read book, sometimes was trying to write something, sometimes was trying to solve mathematic question, kept trying again and again but I was not focusing on a particular work and wasn't able to solve a simple question too.

At the time, I was totally crazy about her. I was not feeling well in reading, writing and was not able to solve a simple question. Her face was appearing in my mind again and again. Whatever Manu told me, talked with me and everything were coming in my mind.

At that time was the month of February and the night was also very cold. Air was blowing very cold too. Despite that I went on roof and started walking, sometimes sat somewhere and sometimes again started walking.

Somebody has said that always think positives but when I was thinking positive then I had got many types of side effects.

When I was walking on the roof and also making plans, "How to meet her? How to tell her that I love you and want to marry you...?"

But I started thinking again and talking to myself, "What am I doing now...? This age is not good for these things and this is the time to build up my career. If she will be in my destiny then she must come again in my life. But if I deserve better than her then I will get and if not then I will not get."

At 3AM, I called Anandita and told her, "Anandita...., I'm not feeling sleepy."

Anandita asked me, "But...why...?"

I said, "I don't know...why...? Please help me."

Anandita understood why...I was not sleeping...

Anandita asked me, "Missing Manu...!"

I said, "Yes...! I tried several times to forget her but I couldn't."

Anandita said, "*I know and can understand your feelings and you know...what...? Our heart is too idiot. The one who lives nearby you and the one who loves you, cares about you, it does not recognize and the one who does not, it wants to run behind and without any meaning and expectation.*"

I asked her, "What do you mean?"

(*I think, Anandita was saying indirectly that she has started loving me. But I was too stupid because at that time there was a veil over my eyes called Manu that I couldn't understand and I was lost in the memory of Manu and didn't understand that's why didn't worry about Anandita's feelings, and without any expectation I was running behind Manu.*)

Anandita said, "Nothing...don't worry...! Please try to sleep and if you don't sleep then you will become ill. And if you become ill then I will not feel well. Tomorrow is our class, if you don't come then I will also not go. If you want that our studies along with you became useless, then don't sleep."

I said, "But Anandita....! I understand one thing and I've known that this age is not good for these things and this is the time to build my career so if she will be in my destiny then she must come again in my life. But if I deserve better than her then I will get and if not then I will not get."

Anandita laughed and became happy to know that then she said, "Doggy....now you understood, what I was trying to tell you."

I said, "Yes...., let's see...!"

Anandita became very happy and replied, "Of course dear, you deserve better than her. Don't worry...! Now you fall asleep."

I said, "Okay...! Yes...! Bye good night."

Anandita said, "So please my dear Doggy, laal-pile-blue-nile...please-please-please sleep now and good night."

Anandita called me again to ask about and said, "Are you sleeping or not?"

I said, "Yes...I was try to sleep but you woke me."

Anandita said, "Okay-okay...I'm sorry my dear laal-pile-blue-nila-pila please sleep."

That day I convinced myself and solved my puzzle of life but I didn't understand Anandita's puzzle and I asked her several times that why did she say like that?

But she said, "Nothing...Doggy....! I told you just like that."

Then I thought that it was not good time to ask her and said to her, "Good night...! And I got to sleep."

Of course, I was telling myself and thinking, "If Manu will be in my destiny then she must be come to my life."

But it was not possible for me to forget her suddenly. I tried a lot but sometimes that pain came out at my face. For that reason I didn't study well. Thereafter, Anandita got to know and she shared everything with Pallavi and Manu.

When Manu got to know about me, "I love her and I'm not studying well", she decided to come to meet me just one time. Might be just like Anandita....Manu also started worrying about me to about my condition.

One day, Manu talked to Pallavi and told her to say Anandita "I'm coming next week."

Manu also asked Pallavi to give Anandita's number, after taking Anandita's number and Manu called to her.

Manu asked Anandita everything about me, but Manu realized and got to know about Anandita that she also started deeply loving me and caring about me, worried about me to see her behaviour.

When I became sad Anandita got sad too. However, Anandita couldn't tell me anything that she kept loving me. But I was always smiling and felt happy being with her.

(*Manu had gotten proof that one day Anandita was saying truth that when she was spending with me whole night and Anandita told Manu and Pallavi that she really started loving me.*)

Anandita called and told me, "Doggy..... I want to tell you some good news."

I said, "Yes...Jangli! Tell...? What kind of good news"

Anandita told me, "Do you know...what? I talked Pallavi some time ago and she told me that your dream girl...I Manu....she is coming."

I said and asked her, "Really..., but wa-wa-what and how...?"

Anandita said to me, "Actually Manu has some work here that's why she is coming and if you want to meet then I can arrange to meet you from her."

When I heard about, "Manu is coming." And there was no limit to my happiness.

Thereafter, I said with excitement, "What did you say...? Manu is coming back. My Manu is coming."

Anandita said, "Yes....she is coming next week. Do you want to meet her...?"

I said, "My dear, of course I want to meet her but not only want, I'm excited to meet her."

Anandita said with a normally tone, "Okay....great....!"

When, Anandita told me that Manu was coming. I became too much happy and was very excited to meet her and I told her, "Okay...! When...will she come please tell me...?"

Anandita said again, "Idiot...! I told you already, she is coming next week. Actually, I tell you because she also told you the day that when she would come here she will come to meet you. That's why I told you."

I said to Anandita, "Jangli...! I....I....I can't tell you how much happy today, I am when I got to know about this good news! Believe me...., really-really so happy. And thank you so-so-so much my dear, Jangli! That's why I tell you, you are my best and my cute angel girl."

Anandita laughed and said, "Okay-okay...! That's enough. I never see your excitement when you meet me and today when I told you, she is coming. Then you are looking so happy and excited to meet her. Now I understood that what is my value in front of you?"

I was smiling and said, "Nothing dear and you should know one thing that you are very important person of my life and nobody can occupy your space."

Anandita said, "My dear doggy! I am just kidding. I know and understand how much you love me...!"

I said, "But please don't say again because before I was just living my life but when you entered into my life, I have known and understood how much life is beautiful and how to live this beautiful life and thank you so much...!"

Anandita smiled and said, "Waooo....! That's great...Doggy! And thank you and now if you tell me anything more then I will tell her to come next month."

I was also smiling and said, "You will never do like that."

She said, "Yes-yes...! Because I don't want to see your sad and rotten face. And don't become too emotional. And now I'm going and bye."

I also said, "Okay Chhipkilli...bye."

From that day, the days seemed longer. Every day I woke up in the morning and used to wait for the next morning, "When will it come?"

One day when Anandita told me, "Pallavi told me that Manu is coming here and she told me that she will come with Manu to meet us next day. Doggy! Are you coming?"

I said, "Yes-yes-yes…..! Of course, I want but you are also coming with me."

She said, "No-no....! What will I do coming with you? I'm not coming with you."

I said, "No-no…..! I don't want to listen to any thing, you will come, and now finally you are going with me, and that's all."

I became some emotional and said, "Dear….! Without you I will not feel good. Please come with me…!"

She agreed and was ready to go.

Next morning, I woke up early in the morning and without doing anything and going anywhere.

I made a call to Anandita and asked her, "When will we go and did she call you or not…?"

Anandita said on call, "Why do you worry? Actually they are going to a park and Pallavi also told us to come at there."

I said, "Okay…when…she will call and tell you to come then please also infrom me."

Again after a few minutes I called and asked the same question.

Anandita said, "No…She hasn't called yet.

I said with a low voice, "Okay…!"

Anandita said, "Oh Doggy….! You don't worry when she calls me, I will inform you…, now be happy…!"

I said, "Okay…I will wait."

Anandita asked, "Did you have your breakfast…?"

I said, "Not yet, I just came from the washroom."

Anandita said, "Dude…really you are too much, first you take your breakfast and just relax now."

I said, "Okay…I will." and put down the phone.

Similarly, I called her not one time but several times and asked her the same question, "Manu phoned you or not?"

Anandita replied only one thing, "Why do you worry? She will call."

Then lastly I said, "Do one thing, call Manu or Pallavi and ask her when she will come…?"

Anandita said, "Okay….dude…! I try to call her and ask about going."

I said, "Yes, please ask and call her and thereafter inform me."

Thereafter Anandita called Pallavi and asked to her, "When are you coming…?"

Pallavi said to Anandita, "Anandita…! I know that he told you to ask whether we are coming, so you tell him not to worry. When we will be ready, I will inform you before 10 minutes."

Anandita said to her, "Yes dear…! Since morning he called and asked me several times about your coming."

Pallavi said, "Yes…! I know that very well. So tell him not to worry, Manu can't go back without meeting."

And After saying this, Pallavi hung up.

After that Anandita said to me, "Now you heard it and so be happy….!"

I became happy and said, "Yes….let us wait…!"

(Actually I was on the conference when Anandita was talking on phone and asking to Pallavi about coming.)

Then I said, "Okay then please call me when she will tell you to come."

Anandita replied same answer, "Okay......! Definitely! And don't you worry much."

I said, "I don't know...how...?"

In that way, I called her each 20 minutes or half an hour.

Lastly, I said to her, "Please call her again just once time and ask her when she will go."

Actually, due to my calling Anandita many times, she was much troubled but was not showing up and did not let me feel that she was being bothered by my activities.

Despite that, Anandita didn't say anything rudely and normally said, "Okay...I will call...you don't worry, let me call her first and ask her when she will go. Just relax now and hold on...!"

Then Anandita called Pallavi and asked her, "Will you go today or not? Please tell me....!"

Pallavi said, "Sorry...sorry...! I was about to call you and..., of course, we will go.... come on. Get ready and come soon to the park, we're reaching very soon."

Anandita called me, I instantly received the call and she said, "Doggy..., Come soon near my hostel, after, we will go together."

I reached very soon near her Hostel and we went together to the park, Pallavi and Manu also came.

When we reached the park and I saw her, I couldn't believe my eyes and I can't tell you, how much happy I was to meet her.

But when, Manu saw me with Anandita. Manu said, "You've also come and nice to see you again..!"

I felt just like, I was unknown for her, I looked at Anandita.

Anandita understood what I wanted to ask her then she held my hand and said to Manu, "Yes... I can't go anywhere without him. He is my best friend."

I liked one thing in Anandita's nature, whenever I used to get embarrassed then she interrupted and supported me everywhere.

Manu said to us, "Woo.....! I was just kidding and nice to meet you especially for Siddhartha because I know your story about me and I really respect you a lot for your feeling."

On the other hand, when I saw her, I was shocked to see her. Actually Manu was married because she had used a little vermillion on her head so that no one could see. I felt too much nervousness and upset then Anandita understood my feeling my situation then she kept holding my hand more tightly and looked at my eyes and through her eyes expression she tried to tell me to control myself.

Then I, for a moment, closed my eyes and again opened, thereafter I smiled and said, "I am also happy to meet and good to see you again and thank you so much for coming."

Manu smiled and said, "You don't need to say thanks me because I am happy to meet you again."

I smiled and said, "But I'm also surprised to see your different look."

I said again, "But why, isn't it too soon."

Manu smiled and understood then said, "No-no..., I wasn't like that. But actually I and my boyfriend had been in relationship from 10th standard. And I didn't say to anyone. On the other hand, first! In my family, marriages get done very early and second! My parents had some doubt about me. So my parents had decided to marry me as soon as possible. However, when they doubted then I shared to my parents about us everything then at first they didn't want that I marry him because we do not belonging to the same caste. Despite this I got inter-cast marriage in the court but I insisted thereafter they agreed. That's why we had to do like this."

I said to her, "Wow...! Waooo...! That's great....now... what... I say now."

Manu said, "What....?"

I said, "Nothing...let's enjoy your new life."

We did a lot of fun together. (Before when we were coming to meet Manu and Pallavi in the park, at that time I just told to Anandita that for just one hour, try to create some situation, any kind of, and to go with Pallavi to purchase and to do anything and leave us (me and Manu) alone for spending some time alone with her. Because, I wanted to talk her, to see with her and to feel with her so that the one hour for me, just like.... I lived my whole life with her, "And I don't know I will meet her again or not. And I also don't want to meet her again.")

That's why, Anandita said to Pallavi, "Pallavi, would you like to take egg rolls."

Pallavi also asked to Manu. Then all said, "Yes... of course but where to purchase...?"

Anandita said to them, "Yes...worry not...I know one place. Where, we (Siddhu and I) like to eat regularly. They are very tasty. And I go with Pallavi."

Anandita said again, "Doggy...! You and Manu stay here, we just come."

Manu said, "Why...he and me?"

Anandita said to Manu, "Actually, there is too much crowd over there and it takes about half hour to come back. Till then both of you sit here and talk. Or yes...! Doggy wants to purchase some clothes too so please help him for marketing."

Anandita and Pallavi went to bring egg rolls and I also said to Manu, "Yes... Manu! I want to do shopping. There is a big mall and it is very close to here. So may we please...?"

Thereafter, I said thanks to Anandita and God also for all. Manu and I went towards the Mall. But that was just an excuse for me and I was so happy because what I wanted, that was gradually becoming true. I was going to celebrate my one hour with my love and I was going to spend my one hour with her.

My one hour with her....

We had gone far enough to keep talking and walking. I started sharing with her the whole heartland, those feeling also that was towards her. But I didn't go to any shopping mall. It was wanted to just an excuse for spending some more time with her.

Manu laughed and asked me, "Okay...by the way, you want to go shopping. We have come so far, but where is the Mall, and I don't think any Mall is in the way, as far as I know...?"

I said, "Please just wait...!" and I raised my hand towards her and said, "Would you like to prefer your hand on my hand and if you don't mind?"

Manu asked with doubtfully, "Why...? I do."

I smiled and said, "You do a lot of questions."

Manu smiled and raised her hand.

Thereafter, I held her cute hand with love and said to come, took her a place, where, there was a bench under a tree and I told her to sit on the bench, as she sat her on the bench and said, "Please you sit here, I just come."

I quickly went to a shop and purchased Ice-cream and returned quickly and gave her the Ice-cream. While giving, I sat like a boy giving red rose (which is symbol of love) to his lover and propose her for making/being her life and say to her, "I love you."

But I was not doing like that. I mean, I was not proposing her. Of course, I sat in the same pose and gave her Ice-cream in place of the red rose. And also I was not saying her, "I love you."

But I had to say her the truth. While giving her ice-cream, I said to Manu, "Manu…..! I want to tell you some truth."

Manu said, "What do you mean?"

I said, "Please eat this ice-crime."

Manu started eating that ice-crime.

I said, "I'm so sorry, actually I and Anandita told you a lie about shopping, it was just an excuse for me so that I can come with you and I spent with you some more time and some adventure moment. That's why I've come."

Manu became little angry and said, "I knew that because when your Anandita told me to go with you to shopping Mall but as far as I know that there is no shopping Mall near around in this area.

Manu said again, "But I wanted to know, what is actually the matter? Definitely something is wrong. That's why I have come with you."

I kept sitting in the same pose and became sad. I put my head down during when she was saying this.

Then I said to her, "I'm sorry…!", and started saying again and again. While saying this and I was trying to explain all things, why I did this.

And I was also looking so sad but in the meanwhile, suddenly, Manu said, "But that's okay…!"

I was too busy in explaining, why did I do all things…? Suddenly I stopped, raised head up and surprisingly saw her smiling and asked to her, "What did you say?"

Manu said, "Nothing…to say."

I became sad and put my head down again and said, "I seemed that you told me something like that it's okay."

Manu smiled and said, "Yes…. you heard right, it's okay."

I said, "What…?"

Manu smiled and replied, "Yes…Baba…I said…it's okay…!"

I became suddenly so happy and started smiling and said, "Really….! You did not mind."

Manu started laughing and said, "No, I don't have any problem. I just wanted to see your innocent face. That's why."

I smiled and said, "Thank God…!"

Manu started smiling and said, "Now can I take this Ice-cream?" and said, "Now you stand up and sit near me or will you keep siting below?"

I smiled and kept smiling then said, "Oh sorry…yes-yes please…!" and went to sit near to her on the bench.

Manu looked at me and said, "Why are you smiling so much and where is your Ice-cream…?"

I replied, "I don't know, why…? May be, because of you." and I put out my Ice-cream from my bag and showed her.

Manu smiled and started looking me and said, "Okay! You don't want to eat."

I smiled and said, "Yes…, why not…?"

Manu started eating her Ice-cream. I asked to her, "okay tell me one thing, why did you deliberately get angry at me? "

Manu smiled and started saying, "One day in the class you talked with me very rudely that's why I wanted to take my revenge and I came with you, I heard that you love me a lot that's why I was ready to come to spend some time with you and like a friend, I wanted to know how you are. Your friend Anandita has already shared with me everything about you, and some things I want to hear from you."

I kept smiling and hearing then said, "Waooo…..! That was great."

Manu said, "I'm so happy to see and know you. That someone love me like that, I was not believing it but when I see you then I have known very well that yes you love me."

Manu said again, "Yes…. you are very nice and I'm also liking you as a friend but it's not love, don't get me wrong.

And I'm helpless because you know that I'm married and I love a lot."

I said, "I know, it is too late."

Manu said, "But do you know...what? You are wrong on the direction. Someone..., who is living for you and also loving you. You just open your eyes and find who God really create for you."

I asked to her, "Who is she?"

Manu said, "Sorry.....! You have to find yourself and recognise her, how can I say? But I'm not the one."

Whatever Manu told me, I started realizing that the same things someone told me. But I didn't remember that was Anandita. So I ignored all things and said, "Yes, but really I don't know. Who is she? Please tell me...!"

Manu also kept ignoring whatever I asked. She changed the topic and said, "I think, we have to go." And she stood.

I kept sitting and held her hand and sadly I said, "Yes I think so and Manu....but please wait...?"

Manu said, "What happened? Just a moment before you were happy but now what happened?"

I said, "Please sit here...!", then she sat and said, "Now tell me...what...?"

Sadly I said, "Manu...actually...I don't know, we meet again in future but really I tell you. I don't want to meet you again because I don't want to disturb myself again and before the meeting, I had three wishes."

Manu asked to me, "What were the three wishes and may I know please...?"

I said, "I think…it worse to tell you but only the first wish, I think…, it's necessary to tell you. Because it has fulfilled just now. And that was, "Actually I wanted to spend with you just one hour and I'm so happy that it has fulfilled.""

Manu smiled and asked again, "What are the 2nd and 3rd wishes?"

I smiled and said, "Just leave it….Manu….! What I needed to tell you so I did. And now it's time to leave. Because, we are getting too late and it is 8:25pm. I thing, they are waiting."

Manu said to me, "No, I don't care, first you tell me, what your 2nd and 3rd wishes are…?"

I told to her, "No, just leave it, you will get angry."

Manu said, "Look….! It doesn't matter, I will be angry or not. But whole life you will regret yourself that why didn't you say to me. If something like this happens, I can refuse it but you won't regret it later."

Manu said again, "Despite that…If you don't want to say, then, it's okay. At the first meeting you told me everything without any issue but now what happened, anyway if you don't want then now let us go."

I was smiling and kept thinking. Manu stood and tried to go then I said, "No…wait! I tell you, please wait… and sit here…!"

Manu sat with a smile and said, "Okay…now tell me and don't worry about me."

I said, ***"You already know about my 1st wish. I'm happy because it is fulfilled. And 3nd wish is that I want to hug you."***

She started smiling and asked, "Okay! Only hug...I think, it's not a big deal. I can do it now."

Thereafter, she started hugging in the meanwhile I said, "Wait....don't be hurry up...!"

She stopped and replied, "Now what happened...Oh yes! But it was only 1st and 3rd wishes, where is the 2nd wish and what it is...?"

I also started smiling and said, ***"My 2nd wish is....!"*** And I stopped saying and smiled.

She smiled and said, "What is...why did you stop saying? Look! Don't put off the puzzle."

I replied, "Okay...I'm telling and ***my 2nd is, I want to kiss you.***"

Manu surprisingly said, "Wa..what....are you crazy? Now, you are saying too much."

I said, "Yes....maybe but it's true and I told you before but you forced me to say.....okay... Just forget it and now let's go."

I stood and began to go. When I saw her, Manu was looking sad and I did not want, she felt guilty then I changed the topic and started saying about something else, asking her about her husband and something more. She also shared about her past. And suddenly, she said, "Siddhu....! Do you have any reason about your wishes."

I said, "Of course, I have the perfect reason but just leave it."

Manu said, "No...no...first tell me...!"

I said, "Okay....I have and these are very lovely reasons."

I became happy. My face blossomed and said to her, "Really....! You are not angry."

Manu said, "No, really not but you have to tell me first, what are the reasons. And what are the reasons of your 1st, 2nd and 3rd wishes."

I said, "Actually, in my life, I see many girls but I never felt and said my heart to like making her as a part of my life. And when I saw you first time and really... you look amazing like your beautiful eyes, your lips, and something more. I mean...yes...you was looking amazing. The first time I wanted to stop myself for you and wanted to talk, wanted to spend time with you. I started feeling about you something different. Do you know what? When I go for shopping at a glance I take whatever I like at the first right. But in your case I backtracked because, you know what..? In this age, everybody says do hard work for making our future bright, focus on Goal."

I added, "That's why...I want to spend time with you, sit together. You know that it's my first wish, that's fulfilled."

Manu kept listening and smiling, kept looking.

I said, "What happened...?"

Manu waved her head, smiled and said, "Nothing...keep saying...I'm listening."

I said, "You are kidding...?"

Manu said, "No-no really not...I'm very impressed about you. Please keep saying."

I smiled and said again, "And I want to do only three kisses because every kiss has different-different causes. And the causes are....

1. ***If you are only my friend then I would like to do only one kiss on your head.***
2. ***If you are more than my friend then I would like to do three kisses……1st on your head, and 2nd and 3rd both sides on your cheeks. And actually…yes you are my more than friend that's why.***
3. ***If you are not married then definitely anyhow I want you to be my girlfriend then I would like to do four kisses….. 1st on your head, 2nd and 3rd both sides on your cheeks and 4th on your beautiful lips."***

Manu said, "That's great reason. What about your 3rd wish?"

I was smiling and said, "Yes…. because you are the first girl in my life about whom I was forced to think and wanted to stay with you but it's too late and I can't force you for anything because you are already engaged someone."

I smiled and added, "According to me…and where I know…Love doesn't mean getting lover by any means, it means being happy wherever your lover is."

Manu started laughing and said, "Yes…! I think…you watch a lot love stories movies and read books too."

I smiled and replied, "No-No…I mean not much but yes…true is always true."

Manu said, "I'm not demoralizing you. I mean…I respect your thinking because not all like you."

She added, "And now we are more than friend, now happy…!"

I smiled and replied, "Yes…I'm very happy."

Suddenly, Manu said, "Oh...yes! We are on 3rd wish so what about it?"

I said to Manu, "I want to hug you because I want to feel you what exactly you are and feeling of love. On the other hand, I want to feel you because I want to know when a person loves someone, when he hugs his lover what he will feel then I want to know this thing."

I knew that she loved someone and was married too. So it was not easily acceptable for her and I didn't want to force for anything. But she listened with interest, of course she got angry but after a while she smiled, I didn't know...why...? So she became more respectful than ever for me.

Manu said after a while of thinking, "Which wish do you want to fulfil first?"

I smiled and kept just smiling, without saying anything. Then Manu looked at my face and she also started smiling and said to touch my shoulder, "What happened...and why are you laughing?"

Thereafter, suddenly I hold her hand and said to her, "Nothing! Let's go."

She was surprised and said, "Okay...let's go."

We started going and silently going. I went to stand in front of her and stopped, looked at her face and said to keep my hands on her both shoulders, "Really.... Please tell me... you don't have any problem."

I felt that Manu minded my words and she replied, "I respected your feelings that's why I told you and if you want to fulfil your wishes...? If not then let's go," and started going.

I started smiling and said, "Hey....! Stop-stop...! Please...stop! Yes, I want....of course...I want."

Manu said, "I'm giving you only 10 minutes…you've to suppose…I'm your girlfriend."

I said, "Of course, I want but first of all I want to fulfil 3rd and 2nd wishes together."

Manu said, "What…? Anyway whatever you want just do….as your wish."

When Manu told me to hug her, I started feeling some shy but thought that…that was my first and last chance so I didn't want to lose that moment.

Then with slow motion, I went close to her and with lovely way held her head on both sides of her ears and, as I was trying to kiss her on her head and moved my lips towards her head then gradually she closed her eyes, I kissed 1st on her head, then 2nd and 3rd kisses both sides of her lovely cheeks and for 4th next moved towards her lips and did my lips near to her lovely lips…..and her lips were like a blooming flower. I was about to touch my lips to her lovely lips but I felt, her lips were vibrating and her heart was beating faster as my wish was being fulfilled.

As I kissed 1st on her head, she closed her eyes, then I did 2nd and 3rd on her cheeks and for 4th kiss, did my lips near to her lips, very closed to her lips, it was about to touch. But I stopped my lips to go very close to her lips started noticing her lips movement, her lips were twitching, my heart was trying to say, stop and kept looking at them, kept looking and just kept looking at those beautiful lips like blooming red beautiful flower, Manu did not use lipstick but her lips were too pink without lipstick, when she felt that I was not kissing her on her lovely beautiful lips then she opened her eyes and as soon as she opened her eyes after that my eyes shifted from her lips to her beautiful black eyes, for which I was crazy about from the beginning.

At that time, I was considering myself lucky that I got a chance to see her from very close. I didn't want to waste my time in kisses. The happiness I was getting in seeing her was not in kissing. Manu looked at my eyes and I kept looking at her eyes, I just went on looking, looking and just looking sometimes at her beautiful pink lips sometimes at her beautiful black eyes.

(*On the other hand, of course Manu knew very well that she was married but I didn't know...why...? She respected my feelings and allowed me to kissing and hugging. So, it was my responsibility that I didn't cross my limit.*)

Then Manu said, "What happened...? What are you doing?

I smiled and said, "Actually I couldn't decide which one was the most beautiful of two....Either your eyes or your lips."

Manu smiled and replied with slowly lovely voice, "Which one....?"

I said, "I don't know."

Manu said, "But you have only 10 minutes."

I said, "It's okay....! I'm not that mean," and I hugged her and kept hugging her.

Manu also kept her hand on my back and started caressing my back and said, "Thank you so much for giving me this beautiful moment."

I also said, "Thank you so much.... I will never forget this moment. It felt like I lived my whole life in these 10 minutes."

Manu caressed my back and said, "Yes... I won't forget this moment and now we should go."

I said, "Yes.... We should go now," and kissed again on her head and said, "Okay...let's go now."

And Manu said, "Let's go...I have a surprise for you."

I smiled and said, "What.......?"

Manu smiled and said, "First let's go."

I hold my hand and said, "Okay....my boss....!"

After everything happened, when we reached there....where Anandita and Pallavi told us to come. We also arrived there.

When we arrived there, I was surprised because Anandita said, "Do you know.....? Doggy......! Today is Manu's birthday and we had a plan for you to give a surprise to you. That's why we didn't tell you."

Manu smiled and said with outstretched hands in air, "It is...surprise...!"

I said, "That's great but why for me, it's not my birthday. So no matter of surprise for me, but again you did for me so thank you so much...!"

Anandita began to laugh and said, "Yes, but we had a plan to not say anything to you about this."

I laughed and said, "Okay....! And nice and genuinely happy to know but I'm very sorry to say because I don't have a gift for Manu."

By the way, Manu (laughing....) said to me, "Yes....but at that time, I spent great time with you and for me that was the best gift. Now I don't want anything more."

I smiled and shook hands with her and said to her, "Many-many happy returns of the day and pray to God from my heart you will always be happy, so happy birthday once again...and God give you great courage to fight your any problem bravely."

Manu said to me, "Thank you so much and you don't worry about my gift. You already gave me your favourite gift. And thanks again for all."

I said, "I know.... great to meet you....!"

And why I was lost my second chance, so after shaking hand, again I hugged her and wished her.

Might be, Anandita didn't want to see all that so in between Anandita interrupted and said, "Now it's enough hugging and kissing, give her chance to cut the birthday cake."

Manu smiled to see Anandita's face then Aradhna said, "Yes...please...Manu...!"

Thereafter, I began to feel shy when they started seeing me, was smiling and I said, "Of course....please...let's celebrating but where....? And I don't think this place is good for celebration your birthday."

Everybody wonderfully started looking at me and said, "But....where....?"

Then I said, "I have an idea if you want then let's go but don't ask where...you have to only follow me."

Anandita said, "Okay...so please let's go fast, I can't wait now."

All said, "Yes please, let's go fast."

I started going and they also started coming along with me and after some time we reached a place where, there were six-lanes of flyover-bridge on both sides, a two-lane road on both sides, and a park like a green belt in the middle. There was a lot of traffic. We reached that place with very great difficulty. The colourful light decorations were looking beautiful everywhere. Mostly three colours are used like…which are used in our respectable National Flag. That was mind-blowing and amazing looking in the dark night. Where, we stayed under a tree.

I said, "Dude….! Now I would like to celebrate her birthday here so tell, how is it…?"

They said, "Waoooo….!" And I started asking one by one each, "How is it..?"

Anandita said, "That's fantastic….!"

Pallavi said, "Mind-blowing….!"

Manu said, "Really…it's wonderful…! I don't have words to explain and thank you so much!"

Anandita said, "Doggy this is not fair. Where was it kept hidden, so beautiful place."

I smiled and cuddled to Anandita then said, "Jangli! Let your birthday come first."

Manu said to look at the moment, "Really…this is great and I will never forget this place and this beautiful moment."

"Then please let's cut this cake now," said I.

Manu cut the cake and ate it with eggroll and cold drink too, and we enjoyed a lot. We did enjoy just like that night was the first and last night for us. But genuinely that was the last night for me and Manu…because…really…I wanted that I didn't want to meet her again in my life.

At the time of living, Manu told to us, "Guys.., thanks all because that was the best moment for me and I can never forget that moment."

Actually when I told Manu that I didn't have gift to give her but that moment was the best gift for her

and she looked at me and told me that the time I spent with her, for her, was the best gift.

Especially Manu told me and also told me that Manu was going to take the sweet memory and lovely moment.

We also said, "I will never forget this moment and thank you so much....!"

Anandita and I said to them, "Bye...nice to meet you. Thanks for coming."

All returned to their Hostel. I left Anandita at her Hostel and I also returned to my Hostel.

Finally, for which I had come to Kota form Bihar, that day came. I had only two months left. We studied hard and help to each other then we appeared for exam.

Chapter-5

College Lifestyle and The Journey with Her

After IIT JEE-MAIN Exam, Our rank came within one thousand. So, we got admission in same Engineering College in New Delhi, with same branch.

Anandita's father came with her in New Delhi, he made all the arrangements for her and went back. She started living in a Girl's PG. I also started living in a Boy's PG in the same area.

First day of our college;

In the morning about 7AM, I called Anandita to get ready soon because that was first day of my college and we didn't want to late for any reason. So we reached the college at 9AM. When, we entered into the college. We heard someone stared calling. I was in brown shirt, so they are calling, "Hay…black shirt! Come here."

I turned and said, "Yes, you are calling me."

There were a group, in which there were three boys and two girls. One of a boy in the group said, "Yes! You both…come here."

We confused and looked each other, and talked each other, "Why are they calling us, let's go to see. What happened to them?"

Anandita said to me, "I think, they are looking like our seniors and asking for ragging."

I replied to her, "You don't worry, let's go!"

We went near to them and asked, "Yes...brother! Why are you calling us...any problem...?"

Second boy asked arrogantly, "Where you from....?"

I replied, "Why....?"

The first boy replied, "Hay...! Don't be smart with me and just answer what we ask."

Anandita replied, "Brother! He is from Bihar."

A girl in the group said arrogantly, "Hay! He asked you...?"

(I understood that they were ragging us. That day was the first day of the college and Anandita was also with me. So I didn't want to create any problems.)

I interrupted and replied confidently, "Hay...first of all, what I tell you...like brother/sister or sir/ma'am..?"

The first boy of the group said, "Why...?"

The second boy replied, "Call us sir or ma'am."

I smiled and said loudly to them in attention position, "Okay...so my dear sir/ma'am, if you want to know about us.

Sir/Ma'am, My name is Siddhartha, from Bihar. She is my best friend and her name is Anandita Singh Rajput, from Uttar Pradesh. This is our first year. It is a matter of pride for us to study under your protection and thank you sir/ma'am!"

I looked towards a girl who scolded Anandita and said, "Anything else my dear ma'am."

Including Anandita everybody started laughing thereafter one of the girls in the group said, "No, it's enough."

I said, "Okay....ma'am then allow us to go."

First boy said, "Wait...!" He asked to me, "Do you know Condom...?"

I replied, "Yes sir...!"

Second girl asked to me, "What is the definition of it...?"

I was about to explain and saying, "A condom is a ...."

The first girl interrupted and said, "You stop."

Thereafter, she started looking towards Anandita and said, "You tell about Condom."

Anandita looked me and hesitated to reply. Then I smiled and said, "Don't worry! Tell them, what is a Condom and its use...? Don't be scared they are not monsters."

They laughed and the first boy said, "Hay...shut up..! Let her speak."

I said, "Sorry...sir, she is scared."

I looked at Anandita and said, "Yes...dear...reply them."

Thereafter, Anandita replied, "A condom is a thin cover and it is used by male partner during intercourse. It will help prevent female partner form becoming pregnant and getting an infection spread through sexual contact, including HIV."

I heard her answer, I was shocked. Then the second boy said, "Now you can go."

Then we became happy and said, "Thank you sir/ma'am!" and started going. Suddenly third boy said, "Stop! I haven't finished yet."

At the beginning, he kept silent and was noticing our actions.

Again the third boy said, "From tomorrow for seven days, both of you have to purchase one condom every day."

The first boy said, "Every day, you will have to bring a different company."

Second girls said to Anandita, "You have to purchase Male Condom and give it to me."

Again she said to me, "And You! You have to purchase Female Condom and give it to him." she pointed towards a boy who told me about different company. The boy laughed and said, "Now you can go."

Anandita said to me, "Let's go now."

My face expression was like, I was confused. So I asked the same girl, I mean to first girl, "Ma'am!"

She replied, "Now what happened."

I said to the girl, "Ma'am! There is a condom for female too…?"

They laughed and the second girl replied, "Dear! Ask to you friend. She will explain you."

I smiled and looked at Anandita. She said to me while hitting with her elbow, "Let's go! Why are you talking nonsense now…?"

The third boy stood. He laughed and said placing his hand on my back, "Nice to meet you! If you both have any problem or help, let me know and write down my Contact Number."

I said, "Okay sir!"

He smiled and said, "Now call me brother."

I smiled and said, "Okay brother!"

Thereafter, we exchanged our Contact Number and I asked him, "Brother! What is your good name so that I can save by your name?"

He replied, "Just save, as you want."

I thought, he was looking like he was leader of the group. So I saved his Contact Number like "Brother (leader)."

We said thanked and went away. After going some distance, I smiled and looked at Anandita and asked, "Jangli...! Tell me one thing...is it true for female condom...?"

She said, "Yes, it is for her too."

I smiled and asked, "How do you know about the condom...?"

She smiled and replied, "What do you thing...and what's the harm for knowing...?"

I said, "No, I don't mean like that," and started laughing.

She smiled and asked, "Now...what happened...?

I replied, "Nothing!"

She said, "Don't be too fast. Tell me what happened...?"

I replied, "I used to think that only boys are naughty but now I have come to know that girls are no less."

She smiled said, "And then what else."

She asked, "How to purchase condom every day...?"

I laughed and said, "Chutiye! They are. I think that they are not able to shop for purchasing condom that's why they told us."

She laughed while slapping me on my back and said, "let's go to class now."

We (I and Anandita) met every day in the college inside and outside, sat together in class, did a lot of fun and went for doing parties.

First of all, we decided to visit our capital New-Delhi. So as soon as classes were off or there were holiday for any purpose, we would go somewhere to visit some good location on that day...like Temples and Tourist places.

By the way, we liked our company and didn't feel bored when we were together. On the other hand, when we didn't meet each other that day used to worse for us then we decided that where to go. But I never felt that I loved her or not.

I was totally confused about it. I also didn't know that she loved me or not...? May be, we were not lovers but we were good.... not good actually we were the best friends.

Anandita cared for me, sometimes used to scold for making a mistake.

We collected some money and also bought a bike and I took a flat much close to her Hostel. Every day we used to go together.

Anandita knew how to ride bike and she loved to ride but I didn't know that she knew or not, how to ride bike.

At the beginning, when we bought the bike Anandita asked to give bike for riding but I was scared to give her because I thought that she didn't know how to ride and might get into an accident.

That's why when one day Anandita asked to give her bike keys then I refused to give and laughed. Thereafter, she snatched the keys and Anandita told me to sit behind her. As she started the bike and she rode the bike in such a way that I had never seen before.

Thereafter, I started believing that she knew to ride. After that, sometimes she used to ride and sometimes I rode and she sat behind to me. Likewise, we went to college every day.

I didn't know why…but it was a lot of pleasure when I was sitting behind her on the bike because she drove very good and too fast.

Sometimes, Anandita would start getting jealous. When any other girl would come to ask me something or if would talk to me laughingly.

One day when a girl asked something to me. Anandita started speaking just anything. I asked her, "What happened now…?"

She started saying, "When I'm with you, why don't they (Girls) ask me, why do they ask you?"

I laughed and replied, "You are totally Jangli-Billi. May be, they felt very comfortable with me for asking because I'm opposite gender."

She got angry and said, "Why…am I looking like an OX with two horns that will kill her?"

I smiled and said, "No-No…why are you saying like this? Actually you are not an OX, you are my lovely cute Jangli-Billi that doesn't kill, directly eat."

Anandita started beating me and said, "If I'm a Jangli-Billi then you are my Doggy." And didn't stop beating lastly I said, "Okay...I'm sorry....sorry....I'm sorry...and never do again...! Let's go somewhere...!"

Then she stopped beating and asked, "Where...?"

I said, "Anywhere...!"

She said, "Okay...then let's go."

I said, "Okay...then sit on the bike."

Unfortunately, when I was about to start my bike suddenly a girl came and started talking to Anandita. Actually she wanted to reach somewhere and she had lost her way. So the girl showed her phone to Anandita, and asked about the address.

Anandita saw the address and read it and looked at me.

Anandita became confused and sad. I was smiling, after about 30 seconds I took the phone from Anandita's hand and read the address, after reading I told the girl, "First you go straight then turn right and walk about 100 meters. You will reach your destiny."

The girl smiled and said, "Thank you so much...!"

I smiled and said, "Most welcome...!"

After the girl went, I looked at Anandita and started laughing, then she put out her tongue and showed me.

I said, "Look! You keep saying that no one asks you, everyone asks me only. You know...why...because...maybe, I seem like, they first judge and find the right person that can help them, then come and ask anything for help."

Anandita smiled and said, "Yes...maybe....!"

I said, "That's why sometimes I can be the right person for them and sometimes you can be the right person for them.

Second thing, they find the comfort zone, where they feel good to ask anything. It doesn't mean that I can help them or you can help them, but you or I can help and send them to someone who can really help them."

Anandita smiled and said, "Yes...you are saying right."

I smiled and kiddingly said, "I'm always right...but you Jangli-Billi...don't understand. First you don't know anything, and come ahead for helping, at the time if I was not with you then you would have told her the wrong way."

Anandita was getting angry and said, "Why would I do that...? If I didn't know then I would have told her, "Sorry...!" and said to ask somebody else. That's all."

I smiled and said, "See...effect of my speech...!"

Anandita said, "Don't fly too much, have to come down too. Let's go somewhere and eat something."

I said, "Yes....because after giving you a good speech, I feel hungry. So let's go."

Thereafter, Anandita put out her tongue and sat on the bike. Then we went to a restaurant and satiated our hunger.

However, I'm also a human so I also felt little jealous when any boy went to talk to her. If I was with her then no boy would even talk to her, but when I was not with her. I saw a boy talked to her and I got to know then I asked what the boy came to ask and say but she used to smile and say, "You were feeling jealous."

I also smiled and said, "Why would I be jealous? I'm just asking."

Anandita used to love it when a boy talked and I felt jealous to see. Despite that she didn't give any value to any boy. But gradually everybody had known that we were best friend and no need to interfere. Because we used to go together, used to enjoy together, either good or bad moment we did fight together.

We used to also study together, making notes, doing work together, and help each other in projects, that's why we got good marks.

Therefore, sometimes my friends as well as her friends asked us for help, giving and making notes and sometimes we helped our friends to complete their notes and projects.

One day the given project was very difficult, but we helped each other and had completed in a few days only and summited very soon. Then a girl came (her name was Sneha Dwivedi) and asked me for help when the class was over then I said to her, "Sorry…. I have to go now, so please you can give me your Notebook, I will do your project and return to you tomorrow."

Thereafter, she smiled and gave me.

I had completed her project, next day I came in my college and started finding Sneha to give her the Notebook. I thought, Sneha didn't come at that time because I searched her everywhere but I didn't see her anywhere.

Actually I had to go somewhere, therefore, I told Anandita to give the Notebook to Sneha. After giving the notebook to Anandita, I went away.

After finishing, when I came back, then Sneha came to me, at that time Anandita was also with me.

Sneha came and she was looking too angry and said to me, "I thought that you have good personality but I was wrong."

I was confused that why was she saying like that. So I asked, "What's wrong with you…?"

Sneha replied, "What's wrong with me…! If you didn't want to help me then why didn't you refuse to take notebook when I was giving you? Why have you wasted my time…?"

I looked at Anandita and was totally confused and unknown about her behaviour and I didn't know why was she behaving like that…?

What was happened to her that's why…I went to ask to her, "What happened to you…? Sneha…! And why are you saying like this, your project….I have completed already and told to Anandita to give you. So why are you shouting…what is the point of shouting…?"

Sneha got very angry and said, "Oh…what is the point of shouting…yes…that's good thanks for helping me."

I said, "I don't know what happened to you…please tell me and show me…what's wrong with you…?"

Sneha told me to wait. She bought her notebook and slammed her notebook in front of me and said, "Okay….great you want to know then now see it, you have done a great job."

When I opened and looked at her notebook, I was totally shocked to see her notebook and thought how had it happened?

And I looked at Anandita. She was silently smiling and showed me like she was very busy in her own work but I understood that all that was done by Anandita.

And she was written in every page of notebook in big size, "**MIND YOUR OWN BUSINESS…..!**" With it was attached the total cost of the notebook, also was written in same pages where the money was attached, **"Kindly purchase a new notebook and do it yourself."**

Looking at her notebook, I started silently smiling after knowing Anandita's behaviour and Anandita was continuously busy in her work.

Sneha got angrier and snatched the notebook, and said, "Thank you for letting me remember my duty and thanks again."

I said, "I'm sorry.... I will do it again. Please don't mind."

Sneha said, "Yes right... after doing all things you say that didn't feel bad. No thanks...!" and Sneha went.

After Sneha went, I looked at Anandita and said, "Anandita...I know that you have done this. So what was the need to do all this?"

Anandita smiled and said, "Done...? What have I done...? She has to do herself."

I also smiled and said, "Jangli...! You will not change.... You are too much."

Next day I did again complete her notebook, and gave while saying, "It may be....my friend had done it so please accept it and submit it and I'm very sorry from her side. She is little crazy."

Then Sneha smiled and took the notebook and said, "Thank you....!"

I said, "It's okay.... And most welcome."

Sneha laughed and said, "What did you say....most welcome...? Next day....No-no...no thanks, I can't tell you again because if you will do it like again and your friend...again do it again."

I laughed and said, "Then next day....may be something different will happen."

Sneha said, "Don't worry...just kidding....but by the way, your friend has taught me a very good lesson, so don't worry about the next project, I will try to do it myself."

Where Sneha sat, there she was not feeling comfortable. Where we (I and Anandita) sat together, there one seat was vacant so she saw and asked me, "May I sit here...?"

I was about to say, "....yes....." but while talking Anandita interrupted and said, "No, you can't sit here. I'm sorry....!"

Sneha said, "But why.....it is empty."

Anandita said, "No....one of my friend's will sit here and she is coming. And so please....!" And she was smiling.

Sneha looked at me with anger and said, "Okay....!"

But again Anandita smiled and said, "Hay...., hay..., Sneha...wait...., okay-okay...I'm sorry....please come and sits here. I was just kidding."

Then Sneha turned and said, "Really....it's vacant."

Anandita said, "Yes..., you can ask him."

Sneha looked at me then I started smiling and said, "Yes....please you come."

I hit Anandita on her forehead with my pen and said to Sneha, "Sneha...you don't worry...! I told you already that she is totally crazy so please don't mind."

Sneha smiled and said, "Thanks.... And I will just come....please wait."

Then Sneha came to sit near Anandita and Anandita started smiling and said, "You are most welcome and I'm very sorry for last activity."

Sneha also started smiling and said, "It's okay...and we can be friends now."

Anandita smiled and said, "I am Anandita...!" and shook hands with Sneha and hugged each other. I too shook hands with her.

And she sat along with Anandita. Gradually Anandita and Sneha became good friend, me too. So that was how we became friends with Sneha.

When my friends invited me any kinds of party then I firstly told them, "Look....! Anandita will also come with me, without her I can't come."

Then my friend requested and told me, "Brother....! This is boy's party and in the party....we will drink, smoke and do many things."

I said, "It's okay...! But she will come and don't worry about her."

Lastly, they had no another option and so they agreed, and allowed us to come. But when my friends knew to Anandita behaviour then they liked and enjoyed with her. From next time, personally told me to definitely come with Anandita because she danced very well and when she went into the party and we danced together. And we changed the environment of the party because we loved parties and did dance together.

On the other hand, Anandita also did the same thing. She also went to any kind of party with me but she had one same condition and said, "Look…! If you are inviting me, it's okay but don't forget that Doggy will also come with me, without him I can't come."

One day her friends invited Anandita and she said that condition thereafter her friend said with folded hands, "Yes my boss…as your wish…!"

Anandita smiled and gave blessing and said, "So is it….!"

And she told every girl at the time of inviting, "Don't ever try to dance with my Doggy."

Then her friends laughed and said, "Why…we will dance and of course we would like to dance with him."

Anandita said, "Then I will not come and Doggy will also not come."

Thereafter, her friends said, "Okay-Okay…..! My darling…just relax…we will not, only you will do."

Anandita smiled and said, "Then…that's right and take-care."

But in between, her one friend said with laughing, "My crazy friends…okay tell me one thing, you go everywhere together, dance together, study together, in college eat meals together but why don't you live and sleep together…?"

As her friend said to Anandita about me and our relationship then Anandita ran fast and sat on her stomach and started beating her and said in with funny way, "Idiot! We are only best friends nothing more."

Her friend said, "Okay-Okay…now I know, you are only best friends, you are nothing more, sorry-sorry….really…I'm sorry."

Anandita smile and said, "Then, that's good…. Remember it."

Again her friend said to Anandita, "But…Siddhu did anything with or not…and want to do or not…?"

While pressing her neck, Anandita said, "I will kill you, if you will tell more about us. So there is nothing like this, we have honest relationship."

Her friend said, "Okay boss…I understood…."

Anandita said pulling her cheek with a sad voice, "I wish it could happen and he would understand but he is too stupid, my stupid Doggy…!"

Thereafter her all friends sat around Anandita then the girl on whose stomach Anandita was sitting for beating, said, "I know that something is going on in your heart about him but you do not allow your feeling to come it outside. Now it has come. And why don't you say to Siddhu…!"

Anandita said, "No-no please don't say anything…promise me but we are best friends and without knowing his feelings I can't tell him. Please you too, don't say."

Her friend said, "But…why…?"

Anandita said, "Because I don't want to, and we are just best friends. It is great and honest relationship and I will only wait. I know one day he will come to tell me."

On the other hand I was waiting and wanted to know, what was Anandita's feeling about me? But one thing was certain that we stated feeling that we were incomplete without each other.

One day, one of my college friends (*He was also my flatmate. His name is Mohit Agarwal. Actually, when Mohit became my friend then after four to five months I left Boy's PG because there foods were not healthy. So I started living with Mohit in a 2BHK flat in New Ashok Nagar, Delhi. At that time Anandita just knew he was my friend and flatmate and they both could not recognize each other properly. But sometimes he used to notice and know when Anandita scolded on Phone and sometimes in front for any matter.*)

We became good friends and sometimes we shared to each other some matters. Therefore, he couldn't bear whatever misunderstanding he had about Anandita.

So one day he said, "May I ask something…?"

I smiled and replied, "Yes…Janeman!"

He smiled and asked, "Okay….Siddhu….! Tell me one thing…., sometimes Anandita scolds you, sometimes persuades with great love for something, it's okay because she is your friend, but still don't you feel that sometimes she interferes too much in your life?"

I smiled and said, "Dude…first of all she is not only my friend but also my best friend. And second thing about interference so when she shouts on me, it seems like I did something wrong and I don't know why….? But I feel good when she shouts and at the time I just keep looking at her face and keep smiling then she cools down and again understand me with great love."

Mohit was smiling, and was listening very lovingly and seriously.

I said, "Do you know….what….? When I get angry with her, and when she is with me, makes her cute face, holds both her ears and apologizes. But when she is not with me, she does video call again and again so that I look at her and she show me her face that she is apologizing by making her cute face. Even if I don't want to do this, I smile. As soon as I smile and my anger subside.

By doing all this, I get a strange happiness, which I can't explain in words but when I ask her what does she get by doing that. When I ask her why do you do this…? She smile and tell me that when I smile, she like it very much and feel pleasure to see me."

Again I said to Mohit, "But When I told Anandita, Anandita suppose, I get angry with her about something, after her calling, I don't smile or maybe I don't pick up her call. So……!"

Mohit was very serious and asked, "What was her reply….?"

I said, "Anandita replied….it would never happen….if it happens……..she knows what it's about that I was telling. But she knows very well and positively said, it will never happen."

I added, "Dude! Whatever you are thinking to see her behaviour and may be you are right on your place. But do you know…what? When Anandita is with me then I don't worry about anything and if I do anything wrong. Of course she scolds me, but she understands me as well as, when I get drunk in any party or sometimes more. She would be a lot angry but also handles me. One of my friends said about a party, actually at the day I was not well and she refused me to take more despite I drunk more after that I started vomiting. But again at the time she did not live me alone."

Mohit was just smiling and silently listening my words about her. After finishing, he replied, "Dude! I'm impressed to know your words about her. Now I'm jealous with you. You are very lucky, I know that things that come easily are not appreciated but remember, you never hurt her." and started laughing.

Thereafter, I also started smiling. I had enough confidence that she would never leave me. So while smiling I kept my hand on him back and said, "Dude...! Don't worry about it and I take care of it."

One day, what happened that some of my friends planned a party to go to a famous bar in Noida. First time, I introduced Mohit to Anandita and Sneha each other. So we were total four friends in the party at the night.

Mohit smiled and shook hands with her than said, "Anandita! You are...good to see you and I have heard a lot about you."

Thereafter, I said to Sneha, "Sneha! Let's talk to both and you come with me to order something." So, we went to order some dishes and drink.

She smiled and said, "Mohit! Who is living with Shidhu...right?"

Mohit replied, "Yes!"

Anandita asked, "What did you hear about me or who said..?"

Mohit smiled and replied, "Is a person!"

After ordering, we just came then Anandita replied, "Who....this idiot....really...?"

Mohit started laughing to look at me than I interrupted and said, "Guys! If your questions and queries have finished then let's feel the moments."

They said together, "Okay….let's do."

So, first we started dancing. I danced with Anandita and Mohit danced with Sneha. Meanwhile, we also started eating and taking drinks. Everyone was drunk and in control but I drunk some more than them.

After finishing the party, at the time there was about 1AM. Sneha refused to stay with us. So Mohit arranged cab for Sneha. Again booked for us, within 10 minutes Sneha's cab had come. Anandita said to Sneha, "After reaching, let us know," and she said, "Okay!" then went.

Thereafter, within 5 minutes our cab had come. We (I, Anandita and Mohit) sat into the cab and arrived within 20 minutes.

After arriving, Sneha also called and informed that she reached.

When Mohit saw I got drunk a lot and out of control. He told Anandita, "Anandita! I think to see his condition, you have to stay with us today's night."

Anandita replied, "What else can I do…?"

First time Mohit saw really Anandita was worrying about me a lot and sometimes shouting on me and said, "I tell you every time that don't drink much but again you do."

At night if she wanted, then she could refuse to stay with us like Sneha but she had to stay at my flat because of me.

She stayed. Next morning I dropped her on my bike at her PG.

When Mohit saw that I got drunk and lost consciousness last night then he asked me next, "Why do you drink so much that you lose your consciousness...? Do you know...how much Anandita worried about you whole night...whole night she did not sleep well? She cared about you and seeing her behaviour, I think, she loves you a lot."

I laughed and replied only one thing, "I don't know...why? But maybe, I keep feeling enjoyment after drinking and second thing, because of Anandita. Do you know...what...? When...she is with me...? That's why I don't worry about me and I know after drinking she will handle me. I think..., I also love her a lot but now she is my best friend so without knowing her feeling, I can't tell her. But we are best friends and don't want to disturb my friendship. I want to live the same relationship. I'm very happy with her."

Mohit asked me again, "I pray to God, you both always be happy but again don't depend so much on someone that in her absence you forget how to live."

I replied, "Dear...I don't know... but why would I worry about future? If it will happen, yes.... at the beginning and maybe, I will be missing a lot but I try to take care myself but let's see. I don't think, it will happen and I truly believe, she will never leave me," started laughing and smiling.

Mohit said, "Okay...let's see...!"

Gradually Anandita became a good friend of all my friends, now cared not only me but also my all friends.

They used to call her sister. Whenever I was sick, she didn't go to her PG, stayed in my flat and served like a mother, whenever I made a mistake, she tried to understand me again and again like a teacher, treated like a best friend.

But one day around 11PM, her friend called me from Anandita's phone and said, "Anandita is not well, come quickly and I think, she has to be admitted into a hospital. She vomited several time since evening."

Thereafter, I told Mohit, "Anandita is not well. I think, will have to be admitted to the hospital."

Mohit said, "Wait, I'm also coming with you."

At the same time we left and arrived near her PG then I called on her phone and said, "We are outside your PG. Please take her out and come soon outside."

Her friend said, "No-no we can't come…Anandita is not able to stand…now she is too weak. You have to be come."

Her friend told a girl to open the main gate of her PG. I told Mohit to book a cab and told the cab driver to come as soon as possible. We entered into the PG to see her condition. So the cab arrived within 10 minutes. I picked her up on my lap and I sat with Anandita and her friend into the car, reached at the hospital and Mohit reached before me by Bick and arranged all things. Thereafter, we admitted her to the hospital. Actually her condition was very serious and the doctor said that we had to stay in the hospital at least 2 days. Because she got sick because of food poisoning, she was not taking healthy food, that's why.

About 9PM, I told her friend and Mohit, "You both can go and take rest I'm enough for taking care of her in the night."

But Mohit and her friend refused to go back and Mohit said, "Don't worry about me. When I became ill then she came to see me and stayed in the flat at the night. So this is also our responsibility to stay here and pray to God that she would be well very soon. Whatever for you, I don't care but she is our sister as well as our best friend so we have to stay here."

Then I didn't have a word to say. I smiled and said, "I don't have words to say anything. As you wish, and thank you so much."

Then I smiled and looked at her friend and, "You are a girl so try to understand. I'm impressed that you took-care her but it is not good for you to stay in the night in hospital."

Mohit also started saying the same things then she agreed. Thereafter Mohit dropped her in her PG and while coming back, he carried a bed sheet and two thin blankets so that we could able to stay and didn't feel enough cold.

When we went to meet Anandita in the hospital flat and when she saw Mohit staying with me in the hospital in the night for her then she became very happy, smiling and said, "Thank you very much."

They said, "No-sister you don't need to say…thank you…! This is our responsibility. So you just relax and get well soon…!"

Anandita had also shared to me many times about the food condition of her PG that the PG's food was not providing to her healthy. She complained about many times but it didn't improve. Then I had also asked her to stay in my flat but she was not ready for staying and refused to live in my flat.

Whole night, she was in the hospital and we stayed with her near to her bed, was taking care of her.

Next day in the afternoon, we took her in our flat and said to her, "From today you are living in my flat, don't need to stay in the PG now."

Thereafter, I went to her PG with her so that she could pack her stuff. While doing it, she told me to help her for packing up her all things like…books, clothes, and so on. Then I asked and kept asking so that I would not keep the friend's belongings. Only then I got a small cloth, and it was new and was not used. I knew that what it was. Still I was showing her and asked, "Anandita! Whose is it…?"

Then Anandita attacked on me for snatching the cloth, but I did my hands up and she started trying to snatch but didn't because I was taller than her.

I laughed and said, "You wear it, it's too small."

Anandita said, "If you do like this than I will not go."

I said, "Okay…okay…I'm sorry..! Take it and keep it inside your underwear."

And I raised my hand towards to give the cloth, then she tried to snatch quickly but I also quickly got back my hand and again she didn't able to snatch. I did it several times but lastly when she did her face like she was crying.

I again said, "You are crying… okay give me your bag I put it myself."

Thereafter, she passed her bag towards me when I put it after she smiled and she started showing her tongue.

After packing up all things she checked out of the PG.

I took her in my flat and started living. Next month, we changed the Flat and started living in 3BHK and I provided her a separate flat for living. Now she knew how to cook food and cook dishes, and before I didn't know that's why we joined a mess but now after living with her in the flat, we started making food together and helped each other in making food.

Of course a separate flat was arranged for Anandita so that she could study well and live freely but occasionally used to sleep in her flat. Every day she came to my flat for talking to me and for studying while she slept sometimes on chair and sometimes on my bed.

But when Anandita studied to sit on the chair, while studying, she used sleep on the chair then I took her on my lap then put her to sleep on my bed and covered her. Sometimes when she studied on the bed and she slept on my bed then again covered her with my blanket.

In that way, we started sleeping together at the same bed, and we slept like a child, sometimes I used to make her stomach as my pillow she was and sometimes she used to make my stomach as her pillow. I didn't know…why? But I also felt happy to take-care of her and our relationship was very pure and clean. There was no cheating of any kind.

Now we were going anywhere and always going together, studying together, eating food together. Sometimes Anandita used to feed me and I used to feed her.

Similarly, we spent the 2nd year and passed it with good marks and entered into the 3rd year of our college life.

Chapter-6

Mission Accomplished

Might be…some of my habits were intensifying with my age and my lifestyle which Anandita was not liking….my drinking too much that she didn't want, I would do. Because of which she herself neither went nor let me go into the Party. Directly she started refusing to go into any kind of party. Still, if I wanted to go…she would say that I would also go along so that I didn't drink too much.

Actually, there was a birthday party of one of my other friends, his name was Shekhar Rastogi.

(Just remember first day in the Engineer College, when I and Anandita were coming inside the college and a group of boys and girls called us and started ragging us. Lastly a third boy liked and shared his Contact Number. So I saved his Number "Brother (Leader)" but because of an incident, actually there was a boy from my college but he was one year senior to me.

When we were in the 1st year, Anandita and I participated in a dance competition in the college on 26th January Republic Day, in which we both got the first prize. Gradually everyone in the college started knowing us too. The boy who was my senior, his name was Vikram Singh. He was from Delhi only and had a group. He was the Boss of his group and was behaving like a rowdy. Every time, for some reason or the other, he was in trouble with everyone. Many boys and girls complained about him. But somehow he got away from it. So, after the participation she came into his sight. Sometimes, when I was not with Anandita, he tried to talk to her without any reason and without her knowledge he got her number by someone and started messaging and harassing her. She blocked her many mobile numbers but again he started with new number.

I noticed that she was looking upset for the past few days. When I asked her then she ignored and didn't say anything because lest I fought with him and created any problems.

So, without her knowledge, I started investigation, finally I found out the reason for his problem.

I also didn't want to involve directly. Thereafter, I called Shekhar and I told him, "I want to meet you."

Then I went to meet him in the college canteen and shared all things. He became angry and said, "You don't worry. Many students have complained about him. He needs to be taught a lesson."

I said, "No Brother! I think...we should not involve directly. He has a group and is behaving like a rowdy in the college. And if we fight from the front then there could be more problems. So I don't think it's a good idea."

Thereafter, Shekha had many friends who were already rowdy and were not from the college. So we met them and planned. Thereafter, we started noticing all activities like...when Vikram came in and went away from the college, when he went anywhere alone and so on.

We got all the information about him. Now we had to execute our plan. Later, in the evening, when he was alone and at the time he had his own car. Then we started following him. There were a total of ten people including me. Shekhar and I were from car and following him 200 meters behind his car. The rest were following on bikes and two bikers on each side. Everyone was in different professional dress and looked like…painters, labourers, salesmen, drivers so on and wore face mask. Everyone was around him with two bikes like…two from the right, two from the left, two from the back, and two from the front. They were keeping going and going. Suddenly one of the two bikers in front applied the brakes. Vikram also started applying the brake but due to high speed, he collided with the bike. After that, the two bikers also pushed from the back.

Then what….Vikram stopped and got out from his car. When he saw that the back bikers were looking like labourer and from the normal bike then he abused and caught one of the back bikers collar and said, "How dare you collide with my car?" and started fighting.

Instantly, the front bikers came and they were looking like salesmen. They asked to Vikram, "Hay….Why are you beating him, you also collided with my bike so just leave him."

Vikram angrily abused him and said, "Go away otherwise I will also beat you."

Thereafter, everyone stood their bikes and surrounded him. They suddenly started beating Vikram for about 10 minutes.

The road was very busy but some of public stood and started looking, some started ignoring and went away. Meanwhile, these 10 minutes were enough to teach him a lesson. We (Shekhar and I) also reached as soon as near the incident place and got out from our car and started asking, "What happened…and why are you beating him…?" and started saving from them.

Then all the bikers left him on the road like that and ran away in the different directions. They had beaten him a lot and he was bleeding profusely, because of it he was lying completely unconscious on the road. We picked up and put him in our car.

Shekhar parked his car near a parking and we admitted him to hospital. Shekhar called his friends and they came to see and also called his parents.

I informed Anandita that I was not able to come. She asked to me, "What happened...and why are you in hospital...?"

I replied, "Do you know...Vikram!"

Anandita said, "Now...what happened to him?

Then I said, "Actually, when Shekhar and I was going somewhere then I saw that he was in an accident thereafter we had to admit him in the hospital."

Anandita said, "Why only you...nobody was there...?"

I laughed and said, "Why are you saying like that...? He is from my college and I think you should have to come to visit him."

She replied, "No thanks, if you want...stay there and take care of yourself. "While telling she cut the call.

Whole night he was admitted in the hospital and he regained consciousness after 6 hours. Then we went to visit him. He was very happy to see us and said to me and Shekhar, "Thank you so much both of you...!"

Vikram said to me, "Where is my phone...?"

Shekhar replied, "I think....it is in your car and parked it in a parking near the event."

Vikram said, "Okay don't worry…if you don't mind…will you please give me your phone….need to call someone?"

I smiled and replied, "Why not, take it." Then I unlocked my phone and gave him.

He looked at us and said, "Dude! Please don't mind, this is my private call. So you both….please go outside for a while."

We smiled and said, "Yes…yes…please carry on!"

Thereafter, we came outside. After some time he called Shekhar to come inside. When we went inside then he gave me my phone and said, "Thank you!"

I smiled and said, "Don't worry bro! Now allow us to go and for taking care of you, your parents are sitting outside. Get well soon and then focus on your studies. There is nothing left in these things now."

He said, "Okay…will implement."

Thereafter, we went outside. Shekhar said, "I think…we taught a good lesson."

Again he said, "Who would he have talked to."

I started looking at my calling history then replied, "I don't know, he has deleted."

At the same time, I called Anandita for informing that I was coming, after picking up. I said, "Yes tell me…!"

She said, "Who is this…?"

I relied, "What nonsense…? It's me."

Anandita replied, "Oh…Doggy! You are….how is he…? I mean…Vikram…!"

I replied, "Yah...he is good now that's why I'm coming.."

Anandita said, "No-no...you just wait there, I'm coming as soon as possible."

I wanted to ask, "Why...you...?" but without hearing, she cancelled the call instantly.

Shekhar and I were surprised and said to him, "Vikram might have called Anandita that's why she is coming to visit him. Otherwise she didn't even want to see his face."

Shekhar said, "Definitely....yes...!"

She came after 15 to 20 minutes and she said, "Let's go to meet."

We laughed and I replied her, "Why us...? You go and meet him. Dear...he called you not me."

She replied, "Doggy! Don't behave like idiot! Let's go."

Shekhar said, "Hay! Stop fighting, let us go to meet again."

So we went to meet him again. When he saw us with Anandita. He became happy and said, "Thank you so much...!"

Then he looked at Anandita and said, "I'm really sorry, sister!"

Anandita looked at me then him and said, "Don't worry...Take care...!"

We spend a few more moments with him and then came outside. While coming outside, Anandita asked me amusingly, "How did all this happen? He has completely changed now."

I looked at Shekhar and smiled then said together to her, "I don't know...how...?"

Shekhar smiled and added, "It's totally a miracle for him," and looked at the sky.

Anandita said, "Yes, exactly! Because of this accident, he has changed. Thanks to God..!"

We started laughing, looking at each other, and returned to our location. That was our secret mission, we didn't tell anyone anything about it, not even to Anandita. We could never forget that mission.

That was how Shekhar and I became a very good friend. He was senior to me but the one who said that didn't call me Shekhar Bhai, just only call me Shekhar thereafter I started calling him only Shekhar.)

Chapter-7

Shadows of Addiction

Because of Shekhar's birthday, he invited us to come in his birthday party.

At the day I didn't know, what happened with me. I think the day was bad day for me. When we went into the party we shook hands and wished. We hugged him and passed him the gift.

All friends were invited...Sneha, Mohit and Vikram too. Shekhar cut the birthday cake, everything was arranged in the party....Soft-drink, Ice-cream, Alcohol, Smoke, different-different dishes.

We danced together in the party, and when Anandita got tired then I asked to Anandita, "What would you like to have... either Soft-drink and Ice-cream or Alcohol, Beer and smoke anything, everything available here over here."

So I smiled because I thought that because of her I could also get a chance for drinking.

But...., Anandita said, "Why...? Alcohol and Smoking...so that you get a chance and can also take. No thanks...only soft-drink and ice-cream."

I passed her a sad smile and said, "Okay...I will come and take."

(At the beginning, when we were in first year in the college, sometimes Anandita also took Alcohol and smoke but when she saw and got to know that I also took too much Alcohol with her drink then from the day she stopped drinking. She started refusing me too to drink and refused to go to any kind of drink party.) But at that day there was my friend's Birthday party. So we must have to go there.

In the party we danced a lot and Anandita was very happy to come into the party and but I wanted to drink Alcohol because after knowing and looking… my mouth started watering. Because of her, I was not able to go and drink but wasn't able to control myself too.

That's why I said to Anandita, "I come to take all things which you want to eat and cold-drink too but you sit here on this chair."

Then Anandita sat and I went, and brought all things with some fast foods like Noodle and kept in front of her.

Anandita said, "Who will eat that much….?"

I brought to make Anandita busy in eating so that I could go in the drink party. So I said, "Of course you…but I will help you for giving company. Sneha will also."

I also said to Sneha to sit here with Anandita, "I bring for you too."

And I brought some dishes for her too.

After eating little more then I said, "Both of you eat here and I just come."

Anandita asked, "Why…? Who will eat all these things…?"

I said, "Sneha…will…!"

Again I told Sneha indirectly through my eye because I convinced Sneha about taking drink little more but got busy Anandita for eating or other things and I promised Sneha that I didn't drink more to lose myself.

I said to Anandita, "Please wait, I just come from washroom and will come to eat with you."

Sneha said to Anandita, "Don't worry...he will come very soon from the washroom."

After saying this that I went to the drinking party, where it was happening and with my friends, started drinking and closed the door of that flat.

After my going, Anandita started worrying about me and said to Sneha, "I don't know where he has gone?"

Then Sneha said to Anandita, "Just leave it...and give him some space, he told you he will come very soon so let him go. He is not a little child. You care about him a lot and so just give him some space."

(I had one bad habit. Actually... when I used to drink first glass, then after two-three glasses, I felt like drinking more and more. At the beginning, I took first glass with mix some water in the drink but after two-three glasses, and when I started enjoying drinking then started drinking without mixed water and Anandita knew very well about my nature, that's why when I started drinking then after two-three glasses. She used to hide bottle so that I could stop drinking more.)

But at that day she was not with me, at the time, in that flat, in that party. That's why I left her busy outside for eating with Sneha. I entered into the drinking party flat where I was called for drinking and started drinking one by one glass, and kept on drinking.

When Anandita got to know that I told her to come very soon but I didn't come then she had become doubtful thereafter she left eating and stood. Sneha asked, "What happened?"

Anandita said, "He didn't come, so I have a doubt, I'll just come."

Sneha said, "Don't worry, he will come soon. You eat first."

Anandita didn't even listen and went away.

Sneha said, "Wait....! I'm also coming with you," and started following her.

Anandita started finding me everywhere in the party and also started asking everybody about me, "Have you seen my friend....Siddhu...?"

One in the party, said, "Your friend....yes I know where he is?"

Anandita said, "Where is he...?"

He said, "There is a flat on the first floor, where something is going on, I think, the drinking party is going on so maybe, he is in that flat with his friends because I saw him that he was going towards the flat."

When Anandita heard about me that I told a lie and went for drinking and smoking, she became too angry.

Sneha told her to stop but Anandita got very angry, didn't listen to her at all, scolded her back and said, "You also lied and supported him for going and drinking. You don't know what he is for me. I love him and this is my responsibility to take care of him because of love he is everything to me."

Her face was looking like....very angry but again Anandita was worried about me a lot then directly came to the flat where I was drinking.

Anandita stood outside the flat and started knocking hard then one of my friends opened the gate. After opening the gate, she kicked the gate hard and entered into the flat and when she entered into the flat and the flat was full of smoke and dim lighting.

The song was playing in full volume and everyone was dancing with full fun, everybody had a glass in their hand with Cigarette. When Anandita entered into the flat, thereafter smoke started coming outside the flat and she saw that there were a large number of bottles lying there.

When she saw all things and due to the smoke, she started shouting while keeping her hand on her nose and said, "What are you doing and where is Siddhu…?"

But due to the song playing at full volume, Anandita's voice wasn't able to reach their ears. Everyone kept dancing, drinking, and we were singing loudly along with the song playing. Thereafter Anandita went and stopped the playing song. Everyone started shouting who stopped the song.

So Anandita said, "I have stopped, someone has something to say…?"

That was the first time she got very angry. Seeing her angry face everyone stopped asking and kept silent.

And Anandita asked again, "Where is my Siddhu, and what are you doing all…?"

They gave her way, pointed towards me, and said, "There…!"

I kept sitting on a chair and I didn't know about when Anandita had come and was asking about me. I was totally busy drinking and smoking. When I realised that my glass was empty then I told to my friends, "Hay dude…! Put more drink in my glass without mixing water, it is empty now."

But they didn't and stood silently then I hold the bottle but the bottle was empty. So I abused the bottle and threw it in the corner. Thereafter, I put out new full bottle, and opened the cap and stated filling my empty glass. Mohit came near me and was saying, "Yaar…. It's enough, now stop drinking."

I stood and went to hug Shekhar and said, "He is my baby…and today is his birthday that's why I'm drinking and enjoying."

Then Shekhar said, "Dude! Now leave it, just look! Who has come…?"

I saw Anandita standing in front of me and was looking at all my activities. I was totally drunk, didn't know, what to say or what not to say? I was not in my own self.

I said, "Hay….dude…look…Anandita has come… let's give her some drink."

Anandita started shouting on me and said, "You liar and cheater, you excused yourselves for washroom you've come here for drinking."

I was not in my own and did not understand what to say or not? But Anandita didn't stop shouting and she started snatching glass from my hand and snatched and threw it away then, she strongly grappled my hand, and told me, "Let's go, now it's enough," and pulled me.

When I saw, she threw my glass and was pulling me for taking outside then I got angry and said, "No, you go and leave me for drinking."

But Anandita didn't stop, I was telling her several times, "Pease you go...now...!"

But Anandita kept shouting and didn't want to go without me, wasn't leaving my hand, so I jerked off her hand and accidentally, a dirty word came out of my mouth. But she asked, "What did you say...?"

I repeated the same abuse again after her asking.

Anandita said, "Do you know...., what are you saying..?"

I said, "Yes...and I know very well what to say and what not to do. So get lost now," and jerked her.

Everybody stood around us and was looking and tried to understand me but at the time I didn't care and listen anything of anybody.

Because of abusing, Anandita got angry a lot, her bound of patience had broken and that was enough for her then she slapped me hard on my face, (I didn't know, what had happened that day, like that I never did before in our life.) But when she slapped hard on my face then I also got angry and slapped her again and again. My all friends came and hold me hard and started saying to me, "Hay...are you mad...?"

Anandita kept her hands on both side of her face where I slapped and started looking around and started crying. Thereafter, she went without saying anything, went outside the flat, along her all friends came out except me. I was left alone in that flat. They went behind Anandita, started going and calling her to stop and said, "Anandita-Anandita...please stop…and forgive him, he has drunk a lot that's why he is doing like that."

But Anandita ignored all things, and said to Sneha, "May I stay in your flat…today."

Sneha asked to Anandita, "What happen, and why are you crying? I was searching for you too and where had you gone?"

Anandita without answering Sneha and said to her, "Are you coming or not…?"

Sneha said, "Okay…I will go. But wait…I don't have key. I gave Mohit for keeping."

Sneha went to ask for key and asked him, "What was happened with Anandita…?

Mohit told her all things that happened and said, "I don't know…how it happened..? But you take her and please take-care of Anandita. I will see and handle Siddhartha."

After knowing all things, Sneha also got angry on me and said to Mohit, "Key…please…!"

Mohit gave her the key.

Sneha came with the key and Anandita said, "Let's go now."

Thereafter, Sneha got out her scooty, started and they went, Mohit and Shekhar came where I was in the flat and I kept drinking. He saw, I was sitting on the same chair and half drink of glass in my one hand, in my second hand, kept three Cigarettes in between my fingers, half empty bottle in front of me after drinking, one full bottle had kept.

Shekhar asked and said, "Hay...Saale...what happened to you today? Are you mad, do you have any ideas, what you've done today...?"

Without answering him, kept drinking and smoking. Then Shekhar called all friends and said to Mohit to bring a bucket of water and he bought and put down full bucket of water on my head then I got very angry.

Shekhar started shouting, and Mohit took all bottles and Cigarettes from my hand and told other to hide it anywhere, while doing that, was saying, "What are you doing...? Today...Dude....Anandita was crying a lot and she went."

I said, "What...and why didn't you stop her..? Please explain me all things, what was happened...?"

He said, "You don't know...what...you have done...today...?" then he told me all things, and said, "That's why, she has gone with Sneha to her flat. She was crying a lot."

Mohit said to me, "Anandita left the party because of you, why did you drink so much that you have done all this...?"

I put my hand on my head and said, "Oh...god...what have I done today with her," feeling regret, "I abused as well as beat her," then I was feeling very bad and sad, felt embarrassed.

So I called Anandita but she didn't received my call thereafter, I called several times again and again but she didn't receive and disconnected my call again and again.

Then I made a call to Sneha, on the first call she didn't received but again I called and second time Sneha received and said, "Hay...., you don't have manner how to behave with a girl, left the girl, that too with your best friend. We don't want to talk now so why are you calling us again and again, disturbing her."

I said, "Hay....Sneha....! Please-please don't cut the call.... please tell me where is my Anandita and how is she now...?"

Sneha said, "My Anandita...shame on you....! Why...., doing so is not enough...?"

I said, "Please Sneha....Please my dear...tell her....I'm saying sorry...I know that I don't deserve to be forgiven but please tell her to talk to me just once."

Sneha gave her phone to talk to me but Anandita refused to talk to me and cut it. I was not enough conscious still took out my bike to go.

Mohit asked, "Where are you going now...?"

I said to him, "I'm going to Sneha's flat."

Mohit said, "Wait...I'm also coming with you because you are not well now to go."

But I refused him to take with me and told him to stay there. I went away.

Thereafter, Mohit made a call to Anandita but she didn't receive his call too after he made a call to Sneha and she received. After receiving his Phone, she said rudely, "Now why are you calling me...after him."

Mohit said, "Please listen to me dear, when Anandita didn't talk to Siddhu then he has gone towards your flat and I'm so worried about him because he went alone and, his condition was not well to go outside."

The way I behaved with her was not forgivable, still Anandita worried about me and snatched phone from Sneha's hand and started asking, "What happened to him, why didn't you stop him."

Mohit said, "I tried a lot to stop him but he didn't and now he's not receiving my call too."

Anandita said, "Please keep calling him after that tell me."

Mohit said, "Okay...I will keep trying and now I'm going to the flat. May be he will come there."

After an hour, I reached near Sneha's house safely but I felt someone calling me so I took out my phone from my pocket for talking while receiving, suddenly the rear brake was applied and the wheel went steep and I felt down, injured my knee and arms too and started bleeding a lot, at the same time my phone fell down.

I was injured and was bleeding. Still I got up and put my bike on stand. I searched my Phone and wanted to call her but my phone was broken and it was switched off. So I got angry and threw my phone on the road and started shouting, "Anandita...Anandita...please listen to me, I'm sorry...please forgive me. Please come out...just once...!"

I kept shouting her name....kept saying... forgiveness...but neither Anandita nor Sneha came outside, because of my shouting, her neighbours, and her flat owner woke up and started asking, "Who are you and why are you shouting here...?"

But I refused to stop shouting and went on, continuously shouting, kept calling (shouting) her name again and again sometime Sneha and sometime Anandita but they didn't come out.

However, they didn't come but after sometime police had arrived, because of my continuously shouting her name, (Her flat owner called police that a boy has drunk a lot and was shouting out side and disturbing the society.) Thereafter, the police arrested me, took me their van and put me in lockup.

When Anandita got to know through her owner and he said to Sneha, "The boy was your friend, the police arrested him."

Sneha said, "I don't know him…actually…he belongs to my college and was following us."

The owner said, "I don't care….he is your friend or not? But he should not do this again otherwise you have to leave this flat. Now take-care…!"

Sneha said, "Okay…uncle…I will take care," and she closed her gate. The owner went.

When Anandita got to know that I was arrested then she phoned (called) to my flat partner, Mohit!

And she asked, "Mohit! Siddhu is there or not?"

He said, "No, he hasn't come now. I was about to call and to ask about him, because his phone is switched off."

Anandita replied, "I don't know…how…?"

Mohit replied, "Okay…., you don't worry. I'm calling Shekhar."

Anandita said to Mohit, "No…wait, I'm calling him now."

Then she called Shekhar, "Shekhar! Mohit is on conference." Shekhar said, "Yes Mohit! Tell me and Siddhu's phone is switched off now..?"

Anandita replied, "Yes...! Police have arrested him because of shouting and drinking a lot near Sneha's flat that's why the owner called the police and they came and arrested him."

Shekhar said, "Oaky...sister you don't worry, I will see and Mohit also come to the Police station."

Instantly......, it was about 1AM, Shekhar and Mohit, without wasting their time, arrived at the Police station. They arrived to the police station and summited all documents and said about me in a polite way, "Sir...he is very innocent and little sad that's why he did, next time he will this not do like this again, please forgive him...sir...!"

Shekhar and Mohit started requesting and Mohit also said to the police, "Sir please try to understand, actually, accidentally he hurt his friend. She got upset, and left the party that's why he went there for apologising. I knew, that was not good time to go there and tried my best to stop him but I couldn't."

Shekhar said, "Sir....! If you file FIR against him then he is a student so that may spoil his life."

The police was ready to release me, and lastly said, "Yes..., I will release but on one condition. When the girl...I mean, if his friend tell me he is innocent so I can leave him."

Thereafter, Mohit called on Sneha's Phone and said, "Sneha...tell Anandita....sir wants to talk with her and ask something about him." And he passed the phone to the Police Inspector.

Instantly, Anandita got ready for talking.

When she said to the police whole things then the police understood and the Police Inspector was very kind, after knowing about my situation, released me.

Anandita took promise from Shekhar and Mohit that they should not tell anything to me about how she helped him get released from lockup.

After releasing, we came to my flat, when I entered into my flat, I felt like Anandita was with me just like before she used to come with me. After opening the flat's main door, Shekhar said to me, "Where do I keep this lock and key?"

I said, "Ask Anandita….!"

Shekhar and Mohit looked at me, wondering. I realized that she was not with me then I became unhappy and was feeling guilty myself a lot.

When I felt she was not with me then I felt alone. Whole night I didn't sleep well, missing her every moment.

Next morning, Shekhar woke early and he saw that I was sleeping then went away without meeting me and he said to Mohit, "Let him sleep well and he is tired and upset."

When I woke up, like every day I kept sleeping and used to wake up her in the morning. So I kept sleeping and said, "Anandita…wake up now. We have to go to college."

Thereafter; when I felt that she was not there and felt very sorry to myself and said, "Oh…what has happened to me?"

Again, sometime I didn't feel that Anandita was not living with me, when I prepared coffee then also brought for her extra glass and said to Mohit to call Anandita to take the coffee.

Mohit started looking my face. I said with anger, "Why are you looking my face....oh for coffee?" then I changed my words and said, "I have brought for Shekhar...where is he...?"

Mohit said, "He went."

I said, "Without meeting me."

Mohit replied, "Yes....actually you were sleeping that's why he didn't want to disturb you."

I replied, "Okay!"

Thereafter, I picked up the coffee glass and went in my flat, then threw it outside of window. At the time I was realizing that how much she was important for me. So I was totally crazy for her and started calling her more than 50 times but sometimes Anandita left the phone ringing and sometimes she cancelled. I also messaged her many times but again didn't even see my messages.

So I decided to go and meet Anandita.

After reaching near her flat, I called Sneha because I knew that Anandita again didn't receive my phone that's why I called Sneha, and said, "I need to talk to Anandita, so please tell her to talk to me just once....please....!"

When Sneha said to Anandita, "Siddhu is on the line and he wants to talk to you."

Then Anandita told without taking phone from her hand and said, "Tell him...don't disturb us."

Again Anandita said to Sneha, "You go down and tell him, I don't even want to see his face again and don't disturb me. Otherwise I will call the police. I think what was happened last night he hasn't forgotten. If he decides to go again then I will not take more time to call the Police."

I said to Sneha, "It's okay...Sneha, tell her, I am not scared of the Police but I respect Anandita and don't want to create any situation that will hurt her...Sneha...you don't need to come now. I will not come again to tell her."

Anandita without answering, she went from there.

Then Sneha said, "You have listened now what you want to know. Now please go away....!"

I said, "Yes...I deserve it...bye....!"

Sneha also said, "Okay...now please don't disturb us because last night whatever you did, my flat owner told me that if you do it again then he told us to leave this flat. So I want to request you...don't come again to disturb us. I will meet in college." And she said, "Bye....!"

I said, "Okay....bye and please take care of her."

She cut the phone.

I got totally crazy about her. I wanted to hide my feelings about her but for a long time I had spent a lot of time with her. And she had become my habit. When, I called her name to do something and to help me sometimes.

Sometimes, I used to call her name for finding my book,

sometimes, for bringing something.

Because of my habits, sometimes Mohit made me realise and said, "Siddhu... she is not here, please try to understand."

I felt sorry again and again and kept my hand on my head and said, "Oh god...what's happened to me, why doesn't she go away from my mind."

Whatever was in my flat, Anandita didn't come again to collect her clothes and books. Then I kept it with great love because I was sure that one day she would definitely come.

Anandita stopped talking completely, what used to be done together with work. Missed her a lot at every time, without her everything started doing alone.

So I neither went to the party nor went anywhere, everything seemed incomplete without her. I was completely broken without her.

When I went to college and tried to talk to her but Anandita didn't talk, started going then I said, "I need to talk to you please talk me just once."

But she didn't stop then I held her hand and told her to talk with me just once.

Anandita got angry and told me to leave her hand but I kept holding. Thereafter, she slapped me hard on my face in front of many college students and said, "You are not ashamed that not once but repeatedly I tell you, I have no interest in speaking with you. Now go away, don't want to see your face again." and she went.

Mohit came and was trying to understand me and said, "Dude....whatever you did at the day, that's not easily acceptable for her. I know that she loved you before and but now give her some time, so that, she can understand you by her own self."

I said, "Yes...you are right, I know it's not acceptable for her easily now, I will be only waiting for that moment when she realizes...how much I love her."

Gradually...I was getting away from everyone's eyes, due to which I also stopped going to the college. When somebody used to ask, "Why don't you come to college?"

I used to postpone by giving some reason with some excuse.

When I remembered and missed her, for forgetting her, I locked myself in a flat for several hours and started drinking and smoking a lot, thereafter, whatever things were in my hand or around me I would throw it, break it, or sometimes injure myself with anything.

But if Mohit had seen my wound, he would have asked how all that happened, so I would have told anyone the reason. However, he was also slowly concerned with my condition. He wanted to save me and somehow got out that problem. Actually not only Mohit but also Shekhar and Sneha wanted to save me and somehow got out from that problem.

One day Sneha angrily spoke with Anandita, "Do you not worry about Siddhu, before you worried a lot. I know he did wrong with you and he was your best friend and so what happened now….? Mohit told me Siddhu locked himself in the flat for many hours, when you (Anandita) were with him earlier; he didn't drink and smoke too much, just little in some party but now it became his habit and he doesn't listen to anyone. Sometimes he injures himself too."

Anandita said to Sneha, "Why are you telling me….? He is not a little child to take care of him. And I don't have enough time for the stupid things and the person. You are also his friend, so go and take care of him. I don't need to go."

Sneha saw her reaction, she said to Anandita, "Anandita! Anandita! Anandita!"

She stopped, turned and said, "Look dear….except him, if you want to share anything more that you can tell me."

Sneha replied, "I understand, but please you also try to understand….please stop him….he is immersed in alcohol all day-night. I'm afraid that he may not start taking drugs. Please stop him. Otherwise, you will lose him."

Anandita replied to Sneha, "Look…..Sneha! Whatever but I don't care and if you want to help then please carry on." And Anandita went.

Then Sneha didn't reply and didn't stop her. Because, Sneha knew that whatever Anandita said, she wasn't speaking from her heart.

Second thing, Sneha noticed that when Anandita was telling to Sneha at that time Anandita's eyes and her voice weren't matching…., and at that time as she was speaking angrily but there was moisture in her voice too, and caring was visible towards me.

Because Anandita's eyes were saying, of course she didn't talk to me but still she was worried, cared and wanted to know about me, how I was, how was my health…?

Anandita also wanted to know, "Why don't I come to college…?"

When I didn't go to college and she didn't let anyone know that she was worried about me. But indirectly, Anandita used to ask sometimes to Sneha and sometimes to Mohit and Shekhar, "Why am I not coming and how I'm….?"

But they (Mohit, Shekhar and Sneha) didn't even tell me that Anandita was worried about me and was asking about the reason that why I was not coming in the college and all things.

However, I realized, "All of a sudden these people are getting worried for me, it was not like this earlier, all this is definitely happening through Anandita."

Of course, they were worried because they were also my good friends but not like Anandita that I felt very happy after realizing all that...really I became so happy and really I was happy to know about it."

Sometimes, Sneha came to see me and forced me for going to College.

On the other hand, Mohit and Shekhar also understood me a lot. Mohit reminded me of old things that how would I take care of myself when Anandita was not with me. I had said to Mohit, "I will handle."

So Mohit said, "Now it's time for you to take care of yourself."

And I also wanted to get out from this problem and that was the dark web for me.

Chapter-8

Fighting Darkness and Meeting the Light of My Life

That was the last year of our college. One day when Mohit was in College, he phoned me and said to me, "There is a program, will be happening in the college just like it was happened last time. Everyone is participating in it, one of which is also Anandita, who will dance. If you want to participate, so you can come to join with us. Because next month of this program our final exam will be starting."

I said, "So…what….? I'm not interested. I'm sorry… about it…!"

Then Mohit said, "Please come… I think… maybe… Anandita also want."

I said, "But…I don't want and don't care…if someone wants or not but again I tell you, I'm not interested."

Mohit sadly said, "But…," and stopped.

I said, "But…what…? Dude! I think…you are wasting your time behind me."

At the time my condition was not well because of it what to say and to whom…? But my friends were amazing….they didn't mind my words that if I said anything wrong because he understood my situation and started laughing to ignore my words.

Mohit laughed and said, "I don't know. I mean...everybody keeps expecting that you should have to dance with her just like last time you did, and that was amazing performance, still they keep saying."

I said, "But they should have to know, we have broken up and we are not talking to each other."

Mohit requested and said, "Just try and have to think about it."

I said, "No...now it's not possible."

Mohit said, "Just try otherwise I have to dance with her, sir told me to ask you. Otherwise...yes, I have to dance with her, sir was saying to me."

He said again, "Look...I don't want to do like, I want.... you do with her. If you don't want but you can come to see her dance."

I said, "I can't say anything right now."

Again Mohit said, "Lastly I want to say only one thing, if you come there is someone who will be very happy."

I asked, "Who is....?"

Mohit said, "I don't need to say anything about. So you know very well and now I'm cancelling the phone, take care and come to talk to you."

For that program, Anandita and Mohit were selected as dance partners. They did practice a lot for their performance.

I realized that I should have to go in the program, so I went. My friends became very happy to see me in the program and they said, "We had lost our expectation that you would come but you came. We are so happy to see you again."

I smiled and kept smiling. But my eyes were searching for my angel...Anandita!

When Anandita came and also saw me but didn't talk to me anything and we had not met for so long time, yet she didn't even smile a little to see me then I felt that like everything was tasteless for me.

Friends told me to sit together, trust me where they told me to sit, after my seat...I mean...next seat was empty and I sat down, started talking to them(Sneha, Mohit and Shekhar) happily. After sometime, Anandita came and saw me sitting next to her seat and I really didn't know that was her seat. My friends started smiling and actually they wanted that I sat with her. But I felt Anandita didn't want to sit with me. So she refused to sit there and started going to sit another place.

When I felt she didn't want to sit with me then I said to Anandita, "Anandita! Please stop...if you don't want to sit here then I think, I should have to go, not you, so please you can sit here."

Again I sadly smiled to see my friends and said, "Thanks dude! But now no thanks....!"

However Mohit said, "Wait....Siddhu...I also come with you."

I said, "No thanks...you sit here...because you will have to perform on the stage. I don't want because of me you will face any kind of problems. Maybe you have to talk something about the performance. So good luck...dude...!"

Mohit said, "Thank you... take care...!"

And I went to the last row and sat down there.

Those who were participating performed one by one. Anandita and Mohit prepared very well for performance. But when at the last time Anandita's and Mohit's names were announced to come on the stage for performing.

I think....they were the last performer. After announcing their name, Anandita reached on the stage. She was looking...., Waooo......, amazing, that's great looking. Then I kept thinking that only her name was not good but also it was suiting exactly as she was. Now a thought came to my mind that I was going mad for Manu without any reason. I was blind that I didn't understand her and without expectation I was running behind Manu.

When Manu met me at that day, she was saying absolutely right that, "Someone who cares for you a lot and loves you too. Whatever happens in future but don't let her go from your life. She is very nice."

Manu didn't tell me when I asked her name but at that day of the program I realised that Manu was speaking only and only about Anandita.

Whatever Anandita did for me, her whole things like...how much she was caring about me and loving me; one by one started coming in my mind and started realizing.

(One day one thing Anandita also told me, when I first time talked to Manu on Phone through Anandita and Pallavi, and after talking, I was not able to sleep then I called to Anandita that I was not able to sleep well then she said, "Do you know...what...Doggy..? *This heart is too stupid and idiot. The one who lives nearby you and the one who loves you, cares for you, and worries about your every moment but it does not recognize it and the one who does not, it wants to run behind another and without any meaning.*")

I realised and it's true, **"Sometime...someone.... actually when and how comes in your life...who cares for you, who loves you...but you will never feel and**

realize but you run behind an unknown without any expectation."

After realizing and understanding these things, I started feeling her importance and missing her a lot, felt like going on the stage and lovingly hug and kiss her. I wanted to say, "I love you."

I became very happy and was not able to stop myself to go on the stage but I convinced my heart, "Just wait and of course, she's yours but now it was not possible."

But when I saw, Anandita reached on the stage but Mohit didn't. One-three times his name was announced but he didn't come.

Thereafter, Announcer asked Anandita, "Where is Mohit, who is your dance partner…?

Anandita replied, "Sir…I don't know… Where has he gone….?"

Then the Announcer said with sorry, "Then…what do you want to do now…?"

Anandita got very sad and started calling him, said to Sneha and Shekhar to call him and just once went outside and tried to find him everywhere that he had gone.

But his phone was switched off and he didn't come then Anandita became very sad and said, "Nothing…sir…now I'm quitting this stage and thank you so much**."** and started crying.

The Announcer said, "Wait…you did a lot of practice for your best performance so I want to give you one chance. I mean…if you have another partner who can only help you to dance. So you can."

Anandita started searching and looking everywhere. When her eyes fell on me, she stopped for a while then spoke, "No...sir...sorry sir...! I don't have and please allow me to quit."

And she gave the mike to an operator and started going.

Then, instantly I stood up and raised my hand, started waving my hand, shouting and said to the Announcer, "Sir please wait, tell her to wait. I will dance with her. Please give me one chance and will do my best."

Anandita turned, stopped and looked at me.

The Announcer knew me very well and he said, "What happened with you and why are you shouting...?" and he told to operator to give a mike to me. And the operator gave me a mike.

Everybody started asking each other and searching me to know about who was speaking and from where.

Then I was given a mike for speaking. I said, "I want to say something...please tell Anandita to stay there and tell her, don't go away from the stage."

Teachers, friends, all students started looking at me and they were surprised too.

The Announcer said, "Okay...come on the stage, whatever you want to say."

But I kept staying on my place where I sat and kept standing. And said, "Sir...can I dance with Anandita...? Please sir...! Please give me just one chance to dance with her..., I will do my best...!"

Meanwhile, Anandita interrupted and said to the Announcer, "Sir...please I can't dance with him. I'm quitting."

Announcer said to Anandita, "Why...and I know him, he dances well...? Last time he danced with you and had done very well. So what's the point of quitting...?"

Anandita said, "No sir, whatever but I can't."

Meanwhile I interrupted and said, "Sir...please wait she will, but now she is angry with me. Please let me finish...!"

Announcer said to me, "Okay-okay...! Carry on...!"

Then Anandita said, "No...sir! Please tell him. How do I dance with someone where I don't even like to talk to...? So I can't dance with him and I'm sorry. Now I'm leaving this stage right now."

The Announcer loudly said, "Anandita! I'm telling you just wait there. Let him finished."

Anandita replied, "Sir....please don't force me to do." She threw the mike, and started going.

The Announcer smiled and didn't say anything again.

I looked around then said, "Anandita...please wait, just give me a chance to say something then do whatever you feel rights."

Our friends, all students, teachers, and Announcer started requesting her and said, "Yes...Anandita give him a chance to say thereafter you will decide whatever you feel right."

Thereafter Announcer said, "Yes....Anandita! Stay there and let him finish."

He said to operator to give her mike again and allowed me to say, whatever I wanted to tell her.

Anandita stopped angrily, when everyone told and requested her and she was given a mike again and she kept looking at me and I kept looking at her and kept saying. So I started saying, "Anandita....I know you like me, love me, care about me....but I also want to say something....Anandita....I love you so much. I'm sorry....please forgive me."

Anandita said, "Yes...but you should also have to know one thing that, yes, I love you but now you don't deserve it."

I smiled and said, "Yes...right, I don't deserve it."

Anandita interrupted and said, "Then why are you wasting your time and these people's time too."

I replied, "I'm not wasting their time. I just want you and genuinely I love you...please forgive me."

Anandita said, "No...I can't."

I said, "Please forgive me, please-please-please...!"

Anandita said, "No-no and no, whatever you say, I will always give you only one answer just only..."NO"...got it or not." and she told to teachers and the Announcer, "Sir, please tell him to go away and he is wasting our time. Now really I'm leaving this stage."

Announcer said, "Wait...Anandita...I don't know, what has happened between you and him but if he is saying sorry then just forget him and this is my order to stay here."

I interrupted and said, "Sir please don't scold her, she is innocent."

Announcer laughed and said, "Oh she is innocent then why are you bothering her."

I said, "Sir...that's why I'm telling her sorry again and again."

Announcer said, "Okay...whatever, now you come on the stage and tell her."

I sadly smiled and said, "Okay sir thank you so much...!" and I started going on the stage and kept saying to Anandita, "Anandita...I won't leave until you forgive me. And I keep saying until you forgive me."

Anandita said, "Whatever but I can't."

But I kept saying and reached on the stage and my eyes were full of tears, sometimes they flowed out.

When I reached the stage, I felt scared, my feet started trembling, the whole body became hot and I was sweating.

Everyone was looking at me.

Everyone was in wonder why he went on the stage without telling. I convinced myself and said myself, "Don't lose this golden opportunity."

I was crying and my eyes were full of tears. Despite saying that, Anandita bowed her head down and didn't want to see me. My friends sometimes looked at me and sometimes looked at her.

So I said, "Look...in...my eyes...Anandita...I'm crying for you because I love you please I-I'm-I'm sorry. Don't know when and how it's happened but trust me now really I-I-I love you a lot."

When Anandita got to know about that I was crying for her and I loved her, gradually her heart was melting. Anandita kept listening very carefully and I kept saying.

Her eyes also became full of tears, her face was looking like she was about to cry. But I kept saying and said, "Anandita...whenever you were with me. You cared me like a mother. If I made any mistake, you used to scold me, you used to understand me like a good friend. So I was addicted of you. When you left me alone I was totally broken."

Everybody silently kept listening like watching a movie.

I said again, "When we became separate, from that day, every day became worse day for me. So I don't want to return to the same life. Please stop me and give me one last chance. I also don't want to lose you again."

After saying this, Anandita kept listening and crying too but was not telling anything. Then I said, "Pease forgive me and just look at this I'm holding my ears for saying sorry…," and started doing up and down to keep holding my ears, on the place of counting. I kept repeating, "I'm sorry….and I love you…!" alternatively saying again and again.

I did like more than five-six times. Then Anandita said, "Okay…please stop now."

Everybody started looking at her wonderfully and started clapping.

Anandita was crying and said, "You don't know…how much I was crying for you, how much I was missing you, a lot everyday day and every time."

She said again, "Now I know that how much you love me. I also love you a lot."

While saying that she began to come towards me. Thereafter, Anandita started crying more loudly, ran and came fast near me and started beating me and said, "You are too bad, I hate you…!" and she kissed after hugging me.

I laughed and said, "Yes…I'm bad but I love you."

Anandita started beating me as well as crying. I kept wiping her tears. She kept saying...., "When you did mistake and you realised your mistake, you know that then why didn't you come to me."

Anandita said, "Where you before...? And why are you hurting me...?" and she started hugging and kissing me on my neck again and again.

(When I reached the stage, we forgot that we were on stage and many people were watching us, but we avoided all things and there was a decorated setting place artificially decorated under a green tree for the performance so I took her and made her sit on that place and I too sat with her. Everybody kept watching silently.)

And I said to her, "I had come, not once but again and again, I was slapped once," and laughed.

Again I said, "But what I got in return was...sometimes you didn't want to meet and sometimes you insulted me and I was slapped once."

Anandita smiled and said, "Yes...I beat you not once but again and again, I will still punish you," to make her face like a little stubborn girl.

I laughed and said, "Okay...okay...you can beat me, as you wish."

She said, "Yes...I beat you...first you annoy me then say to beat," and saying this she hugged and said, "I also love you so much. Please don't leave me alone otherwise I will die without you."

I said, "No...no...no...now I've known that how much your importance in my life. So I will never leave you. I'm so sorry."

Anandita said, "Actually I wanted that you would come to see my performance and if you don't come then I will never talk to you but you told me that you want to dance with me and how is it possible...?"

Then I said, "Okay...you would dance...and I don't come it's not possible. Where you go, there I will present. About the dancing then you just wait and see." And I started smiling.

Everybody stood at their place and started clapping, and started smiling. Some romantic balloon started falling on us, some other things also. Then I got to know we came for dancing not for romance.

I said, "Now...I think we should dance together here."

Anandita asked, "How will you dance because you've not practiced. So how...?"

I smiled and said, "I told you that you just see how to do...I have a surprise for you...?"

I smiled and said to Announcer, "I'm sorry...sir...have forgotten that we came here for dancing not for talking. We are ready to dance, tell the operator to play the song, which was chosen by her for dancing."

The Announcer said, "Dude...don't worry and you've given us a very-very romantic scene just like a movie. Now you show us your dance."

I said, "Actually we were very good friend but because of my mistake we didn't talk to each other and we met after long time that's why it's happened."

Everybody started laughing and clapping and said, "Don't worry...that was wonderful performance you've done." And started clapping and shouting.

And I said to all, "Thank you so much for supporting us and helping us for meeting, without you, that was not possible alone."

I bowed my head, folded my hands, saluted everyone and said, "So thank you so much again and again."

The Announcer said, "Yes…at the first time, Anandita was not ready to hear anything. I'm really proud of you that you didn't give up, and you convinced her. It was very nice and that was very nice moment."

He again started clapping, along him all people clapped too and he added, "Now…you can show your dance."

So the song was played and I danced with Anandita, after long time and we were going to dance together with a romantic song.

We started the dancing. Along the dance the audience started enjoying the moment. After finishing, they started clapping. But Anandita was surprised and all people too. Because without practice how could I did that.

So the Announcer asked, "Siddhartha…you've done very well but tell me one thing, you were not coming in the college. So without practicing, how did you that…?"

Same question was also arising in Anandita's mind and she wanted to know that how it was possible. I saw her face, she was surprised and in doubtful condition. When I saw and looked at her face then I took a deep breath and held her hand with love. And I started saying…..

Then I said to all......,

"My dear friends and respected sir... I know that very well and I've felt whoever is here, is in doubt that how is this possible without practicing.

Actually, I lost my hope that Anandita would talk me again, and would come in my life again. I think....whatever I had behaved with her but for her that was not easily acceptable. I realized my mistake and continuously tried to explain myself, and again and again I told her to forgive me. I was feeling a little strange because I used to go to her again and again but she used to insult again and again. As far as I know, if anyone else had been at my place, then he had gone away from her life long ago. But I believe that if I make any mistake, I accept it and never shy away from apologizing to someone who is hurt by my mistake.

However in her case, the mistake was very big. So it had taken about one year but now she forgave me. Now I want to say Anandita..., thank you so much...! And it's happened, just because of my three idiot best friends and their names are...Sneha, Mohit and Shekhar.

They helped me a lot for our meeting. I mean...just about one month before of this day, Mohit called me and told me to participate in this function. But I refused to participate and refused to come. I think....Mohit shared all things with Sneha and Mohit. Sometimes I used hard words but they are very idiots and never mind my words and I love them.

Thereafter, next day Sneha came with Mohit and Shekhar to our flat for meeting and they made me understand and told me to participate for dancing. They knew that Anandita would not want to dance with me but she wanted that I would come to see her dance. Because they told me that, of course, Anandita didn't talk to me but she missed me a lot every time, her eyes always kept searching for, however, about this, she didn't want to share them and anybody but yes she love me a lot now too. So they (Sneha, Mohit and Shekhar) told me to please come, they started requesting me.

Mohit told me that because of his absence, sir was forcing him to dance with Anandita because she dances very well and without her dance, the function was tasteless, that's why he was ready to dance. Mohit told me...actually when Mohit got to know that Anandita didn't want to dance without me (by see her behaviour) but she didn't say anything to anybody because, before when Anandita used to go any party and used to participate anywhere. We (Anandita and I) used to dance together. I think...again Anandita got ready to dance in the College without me because she wanted to tell me through the dance that she still loves me. But she needed my help (to come to see her dance) to know and to tell her that I love her too.

That's why, one day Sneha came together Mohit and Shekhar. They knocked the door and the door was closed without locked. Shekhar little pushed to open the door and it opened then he laughed and said, "Just see….Our greatest boss is still sleeping and without locking the door so that he doesn't need to come for opening."

After opening the door, they entered into the flat and Mohit said, "Just see…..the condition of the flat."

Sneha replied, "But where is he….?"

Shekhar replied, "I think….he is sleeping in his flat."

I was totally drunk and was sleeping on my bed in an careless way. Condition of my flat was completely worse. They entered my flat. Shekhar entered and he was holding a big box and I didn't know at the time what was in it.

Seeing the condition of the flat, Shekhar said to Sneha, "I told you Sneha…..actually we are worrying and caring about him but I think….he doesn't want to enhance himself."

Sneha said to Shekhar, "Just relax….Shekhar….he is our friend, sad. He needs us so just please keep quite."

And she said to Mohit, "Mohit….please help me to clean this flat," and said to Shekhar, "Please….Politely tell Siddhu to wake up and bath now and try to help him for bathing."

After bathing, Sneha put out a medicine from her bag and gave Shekhar and said, "Give this medicine for making him normal."

After half an hour all things were done. Sneha asked me, "Siddhu…how are you feeling now….," and she told Shekhar to switch on the Cooler, so he switched on and turned it on my side to make me feel and more better.

Then I said softly, "Now…I'm feeling better."

Sneha repeated, "What did you say…?"

I said, "Yes….now I'm feeling better, but when did you come…..?"

They started laughing. Mohit laughed and said, "Now look at him….Siddhu! Thank god you recognise us. My dear we've just come and just look at there, we come with your beautiful gift." He pointed towards the big box.

I asked, "What does it have….?"

Sneha told Mohit to stop kidding and saying anything.

Sneha asked to me, "Really…are you totally fine."

I said, "Yes…I'm good and why are you saying like that. Why have you come…?"

Sneha said, "I've come here because of you and to meet you."

So they explained to me and Sneha said, "If you want.... Anandita to come back in your life again, then all this has to be left and what we are saying, will have to be done without asking any question."

Shekhar said, "Yes...if you agree then we will help. Otherwise take your gift....if you want to become worse your life then, keep taking it day and night."

Mohit said, "Yes...dear we can help you in both situations. If you want to come back from the Dark-Web or if you want to go in the Dark -Web."

I said, "What does it have....?"

Sneha said, "Whatever these're for you."

I said, "Is it alcohol....?"

They laughed and Shekhar said, "Look...he knows...about his gift....!"

Sneha said, "Yes...these are Alcohol...., and these are for you."

I said, "No, I don't want....tell me what is your plan...? I agree to do anything for her."

Thereafter, we (Sneha, Mohit, Rahil and I) built-up a plan that when Anandita and Mohit practice in college thereafter Sneha, Mohit and Shekhar would come every day after finishing College's class, they used to teach me same dance which Anandita and Mohit would like to practice in the College and at my Flat. Mohit told me the steps, and we (Sneha and I) used to dance together for practicing so that I could able to do on this stage, every day we practiced a lot.

One more thing, I'm so sorry about it but when the Announcer sir was announcing Mohit's name to come on the stage for performing. I mean...that was also the part of our plan that when his name would be announced, at that time he would not be there, so that I could get an opportunity to dance with Anandita, and convince her for dancing and could tell her that how much I love her too and all the things, that's why I did and now look at him...Mohit is there.

And second thing, when they came and used to teach me dance, which Anandita used to practice with Mohit for today's performance and I noticed that some steps were common and that the same steps, we (Anandita and I) did. When we used to dance together. Those steps realized me a lot....then I got to know, "Even today she loves me the same way she used to do before. That's why she is using these steps."

Those things grew my hope that she is still loving me that's why she used those steps. Those were the unique steps and created by us (Anandita and I). That's why she wanted and informed me indirectly through our friends that I would come to see and could know that still she loves me.

So I came to realize that when Mohit gave me information about the program the first time, and forced me to come and he said to come, why did he say that, "I've seen someone's eyes, even today have the same caring and the same thirst to see you but doesn't share anybody. So please come because someone will be waiting for your arrival."

Again I realized, "The invitation was not from college side but it was form Anandita's side. She was asking to come and she wanted to know, not Mohit. Because he only felt and told me to come."

Mohit also told me, actually one day police arrested and took me to the police station. They refused to release me but I got released because of Anandita, so thank you so much…!"

Anandita was crying and I looked at her and said, "Anandita…, do you remember the one day when you told me that the boy who come to propose you in front of the whole people without fear. That boy would be best for you. You want the boy who like you, love you. Then it's your dream that the boy would do like this. So I have a great surprise for you…!"

Anandita became very happy and asked, "Yes…! I remember and what's my surprise and where is…?"

Thereafter I put out some things from my pocket and I sat on my knee and said, "Do you want to be…and I promise you, I will never go away from your life…?"

Anandita had no bound of happiness and happily said, "Yes…I want, obviously I want and I love you so much my dear Doggy."

Then I raised my hand towards her, said, "I have a beautiful gift for you," opened it.

There were two rings in a box. When I opened and she happily saw and said, "I love this surprise" and she took a ring and wore it in my finger, thereafter, I wore the second ring in her finger.

Everybody stood at their place and starting clapping for us. She hugged me again about 5 minutes then it was 7 minutes then 10 minutes then I said, "Anandita…everybody is looking us."

Anandita said, "No..., Just little more just once little more.... after long time. You meet me so easily I can't leave you."

Everybody was looking at me and waiting when she would leave me after hugging. I forcefully removed her from the hug told her to leave me now please. She left me and said, "Sorry sir...actually after long time I became happy...that's why."

But The Announcer asked to us to stop and said, "Son, now stop it and do it in your own place. Yes.... About your friendships I pray to God....that everyone...get friends like you. When you were going at the wrong path but because of you, they worried about you, helped you and held your hand from the dark web and showed you the right path."

I said, "Yes....sir....thank you very much to all my friends and I consider to myself lucky that I got friends like you guys....and Sir I request you to allow me that I would like to call all my idiot friends to come on this stage for taking picture together.....please....!"

Then the announcer said, "Okay....do it...!"

I smiled and said, "Thank you sir....and started announcing their name...Sneha, Shekhar and Mohit...my three idiot friends to come on the stage. They came, so we took pictures together hugged each other.

Thereafter, the announcer was smiling and asked, "Okay....tell me one thing....what happened to the gift...I mean....the big box that was bought for him."

We started laughing and Shekhar said, "Sir....it's safe....now and today's night we are going to celebrate great funfairs friendship day party together all friends."

The Announcer said, "Wow, your relationship was broken due to alcohol, and is also patching up with the same. Anyway, congratulation for the great funfairs friendship party....!"

But suddenly I replied holding her hand, "No sir...because of which I misbehaved with my dearest friend, stayed away from them for so long. Now I have got all these. Now I don't even want to see again.

Then Announcer smiled and said, "Nice and great thinking. Well done my child."

I said, "Thank you....!"

Everybody started smiling as well as clapping. The participator got prize according to their performance. The Program was finished and everybody went back happily.

At the same day, we planned a party. So we gathered for the party. Ever since we parted, all friends got together for the first time under a roof and we celebrated the great funfairs friendship party.

When I saw Anandita, she was looking amazing and she told me, "Now it was my turn to propose you."

So she started sitting on her knee. Then I laughed and replied, "What the childishness...? It's okay...! I do or you do that is the same things."

But she did not agree and said, "You stop....!"

She sat on her knee and gave me a red rose and she was looking very happy and sweet. Then I held her hand in which she was holding the rose and kept smiling and looked at her, and wanted to see her again and again, one song was ringing to my mind, "Movie- Ek Villain song Banjaara.............

JISE ZINDGI DHOONDH RAHI HAI
KYA YE WOH MAKAAM MERA HAI
YAHAAN CHAIN SE BAS RUK JAAUN
KYUN DIL YE MUJHE KEHTA HAI."

I was thinking and felt that this song was exactly made for me only.

When Anandita saw me I was smiling to see her then Anandita looked at herself, and after smiling asked to me, "What happened.....you are smiling to see me....anything wrong....?"

I smiled, and said, "No...dear, you and wrong...it's far away from you...!" and I took the rose from her hand.

Thereafter, Anandita stood. I kissed her on her head then she hugged and said, "Thank you so my dear Doggy."

She started crying and said, "You hurt me a lot and you are very bad." And started beating on my chest.

I smiled and said, "Yes-yes, I'm bad but don't worry...dear, it will never happen again. So don't cry, everyone is laughing at you."

When she looked at, everyone was laughing at her then she stopped crying.

Mohit loved Sneha and she too but Mohit didn't have enough guts to tell Sneha and Sneha was well-dressed and was waiting. All kept silently looking at Sneha sometimes and at Mohit sometimes and were smiling.

Mohit and Sneha also looked at each other but didn't say anything, she kept waiting and waiting. Lastly, Sneha stood and put out her Sandal and started running behind Mohit and he suddenly stood and run and hide behind Anandita....Please save from her. Everybody started laughing and Sneha said, "Stop now…where are you running away…., I sat well-dressed from a long time and was waiting.

I laughed and said, "Yes Sneha…Beat him."

Sneha threw her Sandal and started crying and telling, "Just look at me, I'm not looking beautiful…?"

Thereafter, Anandita went and hugged her. Then she looked towards Mohit and loudly said, "Mohit! Idiot..! She is crying, now come and stop her."

Mohit smiled and went near to Sneha. He cuddled and kissed her on her head and said, "Hay crazy….stop crying…! You are the most beautiful for me and I love you so much."

He added, "But when you cry then you are looking like…" and started laughing.

Sneha stopped crying, looked at him and asked, "Looking like what…?"

He smiled and replied, "Nothing….!"

Sneha said, "Okay…not like this….by giving Rose."

Mohit laughed and said, "Oh…dear…I didn't know you want this, so I don't have Rose."

Sneha started crying loudly, said, "Siddhu…tell him, don't bother me otherwise I have also second sandal."

I said to Mohit, "Are you crazy, why are you hurting her…?"

Suddenly, Mohit smiled and put out beautiful Rose and sat on one knee and told her, "I love you so much my crazy girl."

Sneha took the rose and said, "I love you so much my lovely pet."

Mohit said, "What...I'm your pet, Siddhu and Anandita....look at her and tell her to not cell me Pet."

Sneha said, "Yes...you are my Pet."

Everybody started laughing and Anandita said, "Idiot...Pet means lovely."

Mohit said, "Then okay....!" He hugged Sneha.

Shekhar also proposed a girl but she was not belonging to our College, and her name was Madhavi.

But at the time of drinking, Shekhar prepared drinking glasses for everyone and said, "Guys...now everyone pick a glass and enjoy the party," and he started serving to everybody.

I refused to drink and went to sit alone. Everybody expected that I would drink but after refusing, everyone got silent and put down the glasses on the same table started telling with indication each other through eyes.

Thereafter, in the meanwhile Anandita smiled and took a glass and a bottle. She sat down near me and along her all friends came and sat around me.

Thereafter, they started looking and smiling. I also smiled and asked, "What...?"

Anandita said, "Look! You love drinking, I know. You can drink as much as you want today. I will not stop for today but it's not good for every day as you know that very well. I promise you that I will be ready to take care of you in every situation and always. That's what you wanted."

I couldn't understand her opinions about my drinking and she liked or not. She knew that I left drinking because of her.

Still she told me to drink and still I refused to drink, and said, "My dear….just think, with great difficulty I have come away from the drink and that was dark-web for me and come to you. But now I don't want to do anything that will bother you."

Anandita smiled and said, "Look….of course I have problem with your drinking but whatever you said after drinking and you never told me without drink. You always spoke the truth after drinking whatever feelings you have. Many times you told me that you loved me a lot and you had spoken many times. You don't get tired to say like…I love you so much my baby, jane-man, darling and so on, and having said that many times. You had kissed me not only on my head and cheeks but also on my lips and many times. After drinking, you told me always the truth, your kissing, your hugging and your way of loving which made me very happy, and I wanted to hear the same thing from you without drinking, whatever you said while intoxicated."

I smiled and said, "Is it true…?"

Anandita replied, "Yes…you can ask your friends."

I smiled and looked at them. Then Anandita said, "I forbid them that didn't tell you anything. That's why they didn't tell you about it."

Sneha said, "Yes….Siddhu….! Whatever she said, is true. She was waiting, when you came to tell her but you didn't. Do you know….what….you have two problems….?"

Mohit said, "Your first problem…..during the intoxication….you told and did that things, which you never tell normally."

I smiled and asked with surprisingly, "And second problem….?"

Shekhar replied, "Your second problem…., whatever you say during the drinking and intoxication, you don't remember all things after getting normal. Even….if we asked you something about what did you do the last night…? Then you used to reply that you don't remember anything and forgot all things."

I smiled and said, "Ohoo….that's why, you have asked about it several times."

Sneha smiled and said, "Yes….exactly…..! But when you told that you didn't remember then Anandita told us, we didn't tell you all things about it. She wanted that you come to propose her without intoxication and without drinking. And she forbid us to tell you and she would keep waiting for your proposal."

Sneha showed me a video. Anandita was in surprised and asked to Sneha, "When and how did you do it…?"

Sneha said, "I didn't, Mohit did it."

Mohit laughed and said, "Yes….I did and I kept it secret without knowing so that he couldn't watch."

I smiled and said, "Thank you so much…!"

Anandita also smiled and in the video I was saying to Anandita, "I love you….Anandita I love you so much….!" sometimes I kissed her and sometimes I hugged her when she was handling me after drinking.

In the video, during my behaviour they were laughing, and Anandita said, "Yes…..my dear Doggy…I love you so much."

After knowing all things, I looked at her and said, "My dear love, before I enjoyed drinking a lot because I knew that after drinking you handled me that's why I didn't worry about myself because of you and because you were with me. Yes I wanted to tell you many times that I love you but I was just confused about our relationship. But now I'm clear. That's why, I really missed you a lot and love you so much."

Anandita was smiling.

Again I said, "So my dear…you wanted that I would tell you all things without drinking. So now see…it happened. Therefore, now I don't need to take Alcohol and I promise you, will never take it again. Because I don't know after drinking maybe again I will do like before and maybe I will do more than before. So please dear don't tell me again."

Anandita held my hand and said, "I am happy to know that you left all this because of me. I know that all the things happened because of drinking alcohol. Despite this, I was again asking you to drink. I apologize for this and I promise you that I always protect you from the bad habits."

I smiled and touched her cheeks and said, "It's okay and don't worry."

She added, "I also have known about Vikram's matter. Then I came to know why he said sorry to me."

I smiled and looked at Shekhar, "You are not able to digest anything."

Shekhar started laughing and said, "Dude! We decided to get you together somehow, that's why we needed to share."

Anandita smiled and hugged me and said, "I love you…Doggy…! Really proud of you and today I'm lucky all idiots have come in my life."

I looked at all and said, "Now it's enough, let's enjoy. But I'm sorry….without drinking we can also celebrate with more fun-fair. So what do you say…guys…?"

They stopped for a while and started looking at me. Thereafter, they smiled and loudly said, "Of course….!"

I became happy to see their reaction and said, "So what's the point of waiting…? Let's get up and celebrate our friendship day."

Sneha said to Mohit, "My dear Pet learns something from them." They started laughing.

Everybody started laughing and Mohit said, "Yes…let's celebrate because whatever you guys do, she will also expect with me done. So please do fast."

We laughed and said together, "Okay let's go and celebrate."

We cut Cake together and started eating and drinking only Cold-drink. After about 1 year of my breakup, we met again and did great friendship party with full funfair.

Shekhar played a romantic song. I danced with Anandita, Mohit danced with Sneha, and Shekhar danced with Madhavi.

Thereafter, the day we again started living together and living happily. After one month we appeared at our last year of examination, and we got appointed through a campus selection job. We started doing job in a good company. Anandita and I started living together and happily.

At that day, in the party, not only I decided to stop drinking alcohol, but also friends promised to themselves that they would not smoke and drink alcohol from the day because the pleasure of a short time and due to a small mistake, leads to regrets for the whole life.

Do you know what…from our teenage life when we watch in movies and our seniors, but especially in the movies when actors consume any intoxicating things like….Cigarettes, Alcohols and so on. Thereafter we start coping in our real life and to do it regular. In the beginning, we feel enjoy for short time and for show up but, unfortunately, it becomes our habits and we get addicted of it. These habits become such that we cannot leave them even if we want to. Due to which we make such a mistake which remains to be recognized for the rest of our life. Sometimes, this mistake becomes so big that it separates us from our families. It becomes the cause of diseases like cancer and sometimes we even have to lose our lives.

Just think, why should you become the cause of sorrow for the rest of your life just for the pleasure and show up of the beginning?

Hay….guys….! I'm not a motivator and not motivating you. I just shared my life experience with you and may be you know better than me. What's good and bad for you…?

So, thank you very much to show your interest in my book.

www.ingramcontent.com/pod-product-compliance
Lightning Source LLC
LaVergne TN
LVHW041946070526
838199LV00051BA/2919